CAPE MAY DIAMONDS

CLAUDIA VANCE

CHAPTER ONE

Sarah stood barefoot in the sand at Sunset Beach, her toes sinking into the cool grains as she smoothed down the front of her ivory tea-length dress for what felt like the hundredth time. The fabric was simple and elegant, nothing like the elaborate gown she'd once imagined wearing.

"You look beautiful," Chris said, reaching for her hand. His navy suit jacket was already draped over his arm, the sleeves of his white shirt rolled up to his elbows. The afternoon sun was warm on their skin.

"I'm nervous," she admitted, squeezing his fingers.

"Me too." He grinned. "But in a good way, right?"

Sarah nodded, glancing down at the sand around their feet. She could see them scattered everywhere. Cape May diamonds. The small quartz pebbles caught the light, transforming from ordinary stones into something magical. They glittered and sparkled across the beach. She'd walked this stretch of coastline hundreds of times, but today they seemed different. More brilliant. More present.

"Look at all of them," she murmured, crouching down to pick one up.

Chris knelt beside her. "All the way down the Delaware just to end up right here."

"Kind of poetic, isn't it?" Sarah mused, setting the stone back down gently. "The journey they took."

"Like us," Chris replied, standing and helping her to her feet. "Our own journey."

Behind them, their officiant, a kind-faced woman named Ellen whom they'd met through The Book Nook, was setting up a portable speaker. Margaret and Dave had arrived early, along with Liz and Greg, all of them helping to arrange the handful of chairs they'd brought. It was supposed to be an intimate ceremony, just close friends and family. Private. Perfect.

Except the beach was already crowded.

Sarah surveyed the scene with growing unease. Groups of tourists dotted the shoreline, some bent over searching for Cape May diamonds, others sitting in beach chairs or on blankets enjoying the view of the bay. A family with three small children had claimed the spot directly behind where Ellen was standing, the kids splashing in the shallow water while their parents kept watch. In the distance, the rusted hulk of the concrete ship sat half-submerged, its surface dotted with cormorants drying their wings.

"This is fine," Chris reassured her, following her gaze. "It's a public beach. We knew it might be busy."

"I know, but..." Sarah stopped herself. She'd promised not to stress about the details. They'd already tried the surprise wedding. This was supposed to be different. Easier. Real.

"It's going to be great," Chris said, pulling her close. "Besides, look at this view. You can't buy that kind of backdrop."

He was right. The Delaware Bay stretched out before them, calm and wide, with the Cape May-Lewes ferry making its way across the water in the distance.

More guests arrived in waves. Sarah's mother and father emerged from the parking lot, slightly windblown but smiling.

Chris's parents, Cynthia and Charles, hurried across the sand a few minutes later, waving cheerfully. Sam, Chris's son, gave them a thumbs-up from where he stood near the chairs with Harper and Abby.

Donna and Dale made their way across the beach, Donna clutching her shoes in one hand. Nick and Lisa arrived, both of them chuckling about something as they joined the cluster of guests.

"Did you see the ghost tracks?" someone called out, and Sarah turned to see a growing crowd of people pointing down the beach. The old railroad tracks from the Cape May Sand Company had appeared again, revealed by recent storms and low tides. The century-old rails always drew crowds when they surfaced, a tangible piece of history emerging from beneath the sand.

"How cool is that?" Sarah remarked, smiling as more people wandered over to see them. "Perfect timing."

Chris laughed.

Ellen caught Sarah's eye, giving her a questioning look. "Ready to begin?"

Sarah glanced at Chris, who nodded, then back at Ellen. They were as ready as they'd ever be.

"Let's do this," she said to Chris.

He nodded, and they walked hand in hand to where Ellen stood, the sand crunching softly beneath their feet. Their friends and family gathered close, forming a loose semicircle. Behind them, the beach continued its chaotic symphony. Children shrieking with laughter, someone's radio playing Jimmy Buffett, the rhythmic crash of waves.

Ellen began speaking, her voice steady and clear despite the competition from the surrounding noise. Sarah tried to focus on her words, on the meaning behind them, but she found herself distracted by a teenager who had just launched a drone directly overhead, its mechanical whir adding to the cacophony.

"Sarah and Chris have chosen to write their own vows," Ellen announced, smiling at them both.

Sarah took a deep breath and turned to face Chris fully. She'd composed her vows in a notebook last week, sitting at the counter of The Book Nook during a rare quiet afternoon. She'd crossed out lines, rewritten entire paragraphs, worried about being too sappy or not sentimental enough. Now, standing here, she realized she didn't need the notebook at all.

"Chris," she began, her voice catching slightly. "When I think about us, I think about birds." She gave a soft laugh.

A ripple of gentle laughter moved through their guests, and Chris smiled.

"Not in a weird way," she continued, smiling. "But because of your birding tours. The way you're so patient on the boat, waiting for that perfect moment when a heron takes flight or a tern dives. That's how you've been with me. Patient. Present. Always watching for the beautiful moments."

Chris's eyes shone with emotion, and Sarah felt her own throat tighten.

"You make me laugh when I take myself too seriously. You make me brave when I'm scared. You let me be messy and complicated, and you never try to fix me. You just... love me. And I promise to do the same for you. To be patient. To show up. To watch for those beautiful moments with you."

Chris cleared his throat, clearly struggling with emotion. "I'm going to try not to cry," he admitted, "but no promises."

The gathering chuckled.

"Sarah, I had this whole thing written down," he said. "About how you're the smartest person I know, and how you've built this incredible bookstore that's become the heart of our community, and how you always smell like old books and coffee, which somehow makes me think of home even though my favorite place is out on the water."

Sarah chuckled, her eyes welling up.

"But standing here, all I can think about is mornings. Every morning I wake up in our house on the harbor, and I get to see you. Sometimes you're already up, reading in that chair by the window. Sometimes you're still asleep, and your hair is doing that thing where it sticks straight up. Sometimes you're making breakfast and singing off-key to whatever's playing on your phone."

He paused, reaching for her hand.

"My point is, I get to see you every morning. And I never want that to stop. I never want to wake up and not have you be the first thing I think about. So I promise to be there, every morning, for all the mornings we have. The good ones and the challenging ones."

Sarah was blinking back tears now, not even trying to hide it. She could hear Donna sniffling behind her, and when she glanced over, she saw that Margaret was wiping her eyes too.

Ellen smiled and was about to continue when a piercing shriek cut through the air. The family with the three children had apparently lost track of one, and the mother was frantically calling for "Emma!" while the father ran down toward the waterline.

Everyone turned to watch as the drama unfolded, the missing child quickly found—she'd simply wandered a few yards away to collect shells—and the family regrouped with visible relief.

"Where were we?" Ellen asked with remarkable composure, bringing everyone's attention back to the ceremony. "Ah yes, the rings."

Dave stepped forward, holding a velvet box. He winked at Sarah as he handed it to Chris, and she felt a surge of gratitude for their friends who'd shown up, who'd always shown up, through every iteration of their relationship.

Chris took out the simple gold band and held it up, the late-afternoon sun catching its surface. "With this ring, I thee wed," he declared, sliding it onto Sarah's finger.

Sarah's hands were shaking slightly as she took Chris's ring from the box. "With this ring, I thee wed," she echoed, her voice stronger than she expected.

The rings in place, Ellen raised her hands as if to bless them both. "By the power vested in me by the state of New Jersey..."

She stopped mid-sentence, her gaze fixed on something behind Sarah and Chris. Everyone turned to look.

Dark clouds were rolling in from the west, moving fast across the sky. The afternoon showers they'd known were possible were arriving at the worst possible moment. The blue sky was transforming before their eyes, now streaked with gray and purple. The wind picked up suddenly, whipping Sarah's dress around her legs.

"Should we..." Ellen started to say, but she didn't get to finish.

The first drops of rain hit exactly as a massive gust of wind knocked over some decorations. Then, as if someone had turned on a faucet, the sky opened up.

Rain poured down in sheets, instantly soaking everyone. The tourists who'd been casually observing the ceremony suddenly scattered, grabbing their belongings and running for cover. The family with the children packed up in record time, the kids laughing and shrieking as they ran through the rain.

Sarah stood frozen, rain streaming down her face and plastering her dress to her body. This was it. This was their moment of decision. They could run for cover, wait for the storm to pass, try to finish this later when they were dry.

She looked at Chris, who was already soaked through, his hair dripping into his eyes. He looked ridiculous. Absolutely ridiculous.

And she started to laugh.

Chris blinked at her through the rain, confusion crossing his features for just a moment before he joined in. Deep, genuine laughter that bent him at the waist.

"Are you two okay?" Ellen shouted over the sound of the downpour, her nice outfit completely ruined.

"We're perfect!" Sarah yelled back. "Keep going! Finish it!"

Ellen looked at them both like they might be crazy, but then her face broke into a wide grin. "You're sure?"

"Absolutely!" Chris said, pulling Sarah against him. "We're not stopping now."

Their friends and family, who had instinctively started moving toward shelter, stopped and turned back. Margaret caught Sarah's eye and gave her an enthusiastic thumbs-up. Dave was grinning like this was the best entertainment he'd had all year. Sam had his phone out, recording the whole thing.

Ellen cleared her throat, rain dripping from her nose, and skipped straight to the end. "Then by the power vested in me by the state of New Jersey, I now pronounce you husband and wife! You may kiss!"

Chris didn't wait for any further instruction. He cupped Sarah's face in his hands and kissed her, both of them smiling through their laughter, rain streaming down their faces. Their witnesses burst into applause and cheers, soaked to the bone and beaming.

When they finally pulled apart, Sarah looked around at their friends and family, all of them drenched and beaming.

Chris squeezed her hand.

They stood there for another moment, just the two of them in their small circle of light, while the rain continued to pour and their guests whooped and hollered around them. Sarah's carefully styled hair hung in wet ropes down her back. Chris's suit would probably never recover. The setup they'd arranged so carefully was completely destroyed.

And it was perfect.

"Alright, married people!" Margaret called out, struggling to be heard over the rain. "How about we get out of this weather before we all drown?"

"Chalfonte!" Liz shouted. "Everyone to Chalfonte!"

The group dispersed quickly, everyone making a soggy dash for their cars. Sarah and Chris walked back across the beach together, hand in hand.

By the time they reached Chris's truck, Sarah climbed inside and kicked off her sandy, wet shoes with relief.

"So," Chris ventured, backing out of the parking spot, "we're married."

"We're married," Sarah repeated, the words feeling foreign and wonderful on her tongue.

* * *

The Chalfonte Hotel sprawled across nearly an entire block, its Victorian architecture a testament to another time. Sarah had always loved the place—the wide porches lined with rocking chairs, the unhurried warmth of the staff, the way staying here felt like stepping back into a simpler era where summer meant lazy afternoons and good conversation.

Tonight, even still soaked, she felt that same sense of timeless charm as they pulled up to the front.

"I called ahead," Margaret offered, materializing at their car window with an umbrella. "Told them we might need some towels."

"You're a lifesaver," Sarah replied, accepting the umbrella and climbing out.

The rain had slowed to a steady drizzle, and as they made their way up the steps to the main entrance, Sarah could see that the porch was already set up for their reception. Small cocktail tables dotted the space, and she spotted the band, a jazz trio they'd hired, ready to play in a dry corner.

Someone had clearly scrambled to move things under cover when the rain started, and Sarah felt a rush of gratitude for whoever had taken charge.

More guests were arriving now, everyone in various states

of dampness. The Chalfonte staff swooped in with stacks of towels, and soon the porch was filled with people toweling off their hair and wringing out their clothes while chuckling about the absurdity of it all.

A waiter circulated with a tray of champagne, and Sarah gratefully accepted a glass. The bubbles tickled her nose, and she took a long sip, feeling the jitters of the day finally start to ease from her shoulders.

"To the bride and groom!" someone called out, and glasses were lifted throughout the crowd.

Chris slipped his arm around Sarah's waist, drawing her against him. "Speech?" he murmured.

"Oh no," she whispered back. "Let's just... be here."

He smiled. "Works for me."

The band started playing, a mellow jazz number that somehow fit perfectly with the patter of rain and the soft light of the string lights. Servers emerged from inside carrying trays of hors d'oeuvres. Bacon-wrapped dates, crab cakes, bruschetta, all the things Sarah and Chris had agonized over choosing months ago.

"These are incredible," Liz exclaimed, materializing at Sarah's elbow with a plate piled high. "You have to try the crab cakes."

Sarah took one, savoring the delicate buttery flavor. "Definitely worth the price."

Liz smiled and squeezed her arm before disappearing back into the crowd.

The rain finally stopped, leaving everything fresh and clean. The air smelled of wet wood and blooming flowers. The band shifted into a more upbeat number, and Sarah watched as the bassist leaned into a solo, fingers dancing across the strings. The drummer brushed the cymbals with easy grace while the keyboardist's hands moved in fluid arcs across the keys.

The music drifted out into the warm Cape May evening,

carrying across the lawn and down the block. Sarah noticed a couple walking their dog pause at the edge of the property, swaying slightly to the rhythm. A few hotel guests settled into rocking chairs at the far end of the porch, keeping a respectful distance but clearly enjoying the music.

"Looks like we're drawing a crowd," Chris murmured in her ear, nodding toward the growing number of people gathering on the lawn.

More locals arrived, some bringing their own folding chairs, others content to stand and listen. A few climbed the porch steps tentatively, as if testing whether they'd be turned away.

Margaret caught Sarah's eye and beamed, gesturing them forward. "Come on up! The more the merrier!"

The band launched into an upbeat swing number, and suddenly the porch came alive. Wedding guests and Cape May locals mingled together, swaying to the lively rhythm. An older man in a worn baseball cap asked Sarah's aunt to dance, and she laughed, accepting his hand. Sam, Harper, and Abby were teaching some local kids a silly dance move they'd apparently invented on the spot.

Sarah found herself pulled into a dance by a woman who introduced herself as a longtime Chalfonte regular. "I've seen a lot of weddings here," the woman said, spinning gracefully, "but never one quite like this!"

The jazz trio seemed energized by the expanding audience, playing with even more enthusiasm. They moved through their set list—classics and contemporary jazz, everything from Duke Ellington to modern arrangements that got everyone moving. Between songs, the keyboardist would call out dedications, and soon guests were requesting songs for the bride and groom.

Chris came to Sarah's side with two fresh glasses of champagne. "Having fun?"

"This is wonderful," she said, watching the scene unfold around them. The string lights illuminated the crowded porch.

Laughter bubbled up from different corners. Someone had brought out more chairs from inside, and elderly locals sat tapping their feet while younger couples danced in the spaces between.

As the party continued, the Chalfonte staff moved seamlessly through the crowd, offering drinks and hors d'oeuvres to the wedding guests, creating an easy, joyful atmosphere that felt less like a formal reception and more like the best kind of neighborhood celebration.

Dave and Margaret were dancing near the railing, both of them laughing at something. Sarah's father had struck up a conversation with a group of locals about the best fishing spots. Harper and Abby were teaching Sam some dance moves while a cluster of amused adults watched.

The porch party continued for a while longer, the music and laughter filling the warm evening air. Soon, the crowd was called inside to the Magnolia Room for dinner. Sarah had been to the Magnolia Room for breakfast before, but she'd never seen it set up like this for an evening event. Tables were arranged with white linens and candles, and the room had a warm, elegant Southern charm that felt ideal for the occasion.

They'd kept the guest list intimate, so all fit comfortably. Sarah and Chris were seated at a table with their parents, Sam, and other family members, and as people found their seats, Sarah felt that same sense of rightness settle over her. These were her people. Every person in this room had rallied for them, had celebrated their love story.

Dinner was served. A choice of the Magnolia Room's famous Southern fried chicken or fresh fish, both cooked to perfection. Sarah had thought she was too anxious to eat, but the moment the food arrived, she realized she was starving. She and Chris had skipped lunch in their pre-wedding excitement, and now she found herself savoring every bite of the crispy, expertly seasoned chicken.

After dinner, the tables were cleared. A different band was

already set up in the corner of the room, ready for dancing. Sarah felt a flutter of nerves about the first dance. They'd practiced this, kind of, in their living room with Chris's phone playing music.

The opening notes of "Baby, I Love Your Way" by Peter Frampton filled the room, and Chris stood, offering her his hand. "Ready?"

"Always," she replied, letting him lead her onto the makeshift dance floor.

They swayed together to the music. Other couples joined them on the floor, and soon the room was full of moving bodies, all dancing and laughing. The band transitioned into more upbeat numbers, and Sarah stayed close to Chris, giggling as they moved to the faster tempo. Around them, guests spun and twirled, calling out congratulations and well-wishes.

Hours passed in a blur of music and laughter, cake cutting —a simple vanilla cake with raspberry filling that was better than Sarah had imagined—and more champagne than she probably should have drunk. Sarah had long since abandoned her heels, moving barefoot on the polished wood floor.

It was nearly midnight when the reception ended, the group heading out to the parking area together. Their guests threw flower petals as Sarah and Chris walked to the truck, the petals sticking to their clothes.

"Happy?" Chris asked as they climbed in.

Sarah looked back at the Chalfonte, at its Victorian silhouette against the night sky. She thought about the rain-soaked ceremony, about all the perfect imperfections of the day.

"So happy," she whispered.

Chris started the engine, and they drove through the quiet streets of Cape May toward their house on the harbor. Sarah rested her head against the window, watching the familiar landmarks pass by. The Book Nook, dark and locked up for the night. The corner where they'd once gotten lost trying to find a restaurant on their second date.

All of it part of their story now. All of it woven into the fabric of who they were becoming together.

When they pulled into their driveway, Sarah stayed seated for a moment, looking at Chris in the dim light from the dashboard.

"The excitement doesn't stop here. Get ready for the honeymoon of our dreams in New Orleans," she said excitedly.

CHAPTER TWO

In the newly converted Furnish & Feast, Liz stood behind the counter, watching the handful of customers browsing through her thoughtfully arranged space. The water damage they'd discovered in March had pushed their opening back by weeks, requiring them to gut and replace a whole section of flooring. But today was opening day, and it had been worth the wait. They'd decided against a big promotional push. No ads in the local paper, no social media campaign, just a simple "Now Open" sign in the window and some flyers posted around town.

The space looked nothing like it had when they'd first bought it. What had once been Heirloom restaurant, a place that held so many memories for them, had been completely transformed. The main area was now divided into two distinct but complementary sections.

On the left side, Liz's vision had come to life, an environment that felt like stepping into a sun-drenched dream. Reclaimed wood shelves lined the exposed brick walls, displaying her carefully assembled collection. Battery-operated taper candles flickered in tarnished brass candle holders while tea lights glowed softly inside amber glass fairy lamps she'd found at estate sales. The ambient light mixed with natural light from the tall windows, creating an atmosphere that was part seaside cottage, part curated gallery, part secret garden.

One entire wall was dedicated to her "ribbon wall," with dozens of spools of ribbon in every color and pattern imaginable, mounted on a custom-built display that looked like a piece of art. The other shelves held an eclectic mix: silk hydrangeas and peonies in shades of blush and cream arranged in classic milk glass pitchers, marine throw pillows in sun-bleached blues and sandy neutrals with hand-embroidered anchors and sailboats, nautical rope-wrapped candlesticks tied with little bows, and small treasures she'd thrifted for resale, including tarnished silver trays that caught the light, mercury glass vases in rose gold and champagne, delicate porcelain teacups hand-painted with violets and forget-me-nots. Freshly picked flowers sat in vintage bottles on every surface: daisies, lavender sprigs, white roses just beginning to open. Throughout the room, her restored furniture pieces were artfully arranged. Vintage armchairs she had reupholstered in fresh fabrics with scalloped edges and covered buttons, mid-century dressers she had refinished to a smooth perfection and topped with ornate brass pulls she'd found at flea markets, antique side tables with good bones that she had brought back to life and dressed with lace doilies and stacks of old hardcover books. The effect was transportive, like wandering through a dreamy seaside grandmother's attic where every object had a story, and where everything, from the pearl-handled letter opener to the silk kimono draped over a dressing screen, seemed to whisper of garden parties and love letters and lazy summer afternoons.

On the right side of the space, Greg's café was taking shape. After his burnout from running his previous restaurant, he'd been adamant about creating something more manageable this time around. The sixty-hour weeks, the constant pressure, the feeling that the work was consuming his entire life were all behind him now.

The café was deliberately small and simple. A compact kitchen behind a beautiful marble-topped counter, a restored espresso machine he'd found through an online auction, a selective menu that changed with the seasons. Greg's sandwiches were built on house-baked focaccia and sourdough, things like roasted turkey with cranberry aioli and arugula, or his signature roasted vegetable panini with homemade basil pesto and fresh mozzarella. The salads were composed rather than tossed: summer quinoa with grilled peaches and mint, or Mediterranean farro with preserved lemon. And twice a week, he'd offer a soup. Currently that meant a chilled cucumber and dill, or a spring pea with mint. There would be eight small tables with vintage chairs that Liz had refinished, and a charming outdoor seating area with bistro tables and string lights.

Greg felt the beauty of this setup was that he wasn't trying to be everything to everyone. It was a small menu of things he did really well, limited hours so they could actually have a life, and prices that reflected quality ingredients without being pretentious about it.

The café featured rustic bread bins displaying fresh-baked goods and a chalkboard menu that Greg had lettered himself. He'd learned hard lessons from his restaurant days, and this time he was doing it right.

The first few hours were quiet. A handful of customers trickled in, mostly curious locals who'd been watching the renovation progress. They bought coffee, admired the furniture, asked questions about Liz's restoration process. A woman in her sixties spent twenty minutes examining the ribbon wall, pointing out patterns to her companion. A younger couple lingered by the fresh flowers, whispering to each other about their upcoming wedding. One woman bought a refinished side table that Liz had painted in a soft sage green.

"It's perfect for my guest room," the woman said, running her hand along the smooth surface. "And I love knowing the story behind it, that it was given new life. Honestly, this whole place feels like it should be in a magazine. It's so—" She paused, looking around. "So special."

By late morning, the pace had slowed considerably. The bell above the door chimed, and she looked up from the Victorian chair she was reupholstering to see a man enter. He was probably in his thirties, dressed casually in jeans and a fitted T-shirt, with an expensive-looking camera hanging from his neck. He paused just inside the door, looking around with an expression of surprised delight.

"Whoa," he said to no one in particular. "This place is amazing."

Greg emerged from the kitchen, wiping his hands on a towel. "Welcome to Furnish & Feast. Can I help you with something?"

"Bathroom?" the man asked apologetically. "I've been walking around Cape May all morning and really need to—"

"Right through there," Greg said, pointing toward the back corner.

The man hurried off, and Liz and Greg exchanged amused glances. But when the man emerged a few minutes later, instead of heading for the door, he stopped and really looked around. His eyes traveled from the ribbon wall to the fresh flowers, to the silk kimono draped artfully over the screen.

"I mean, wow," he said, shaking his head slowly. "The aesthetic is incredible. It's like..." He paused, searching for words. "It's like if a French country house and a New England beach cottage had a baby and that baby grew up to be impossibly chic. The way you've mixed the furniture restoration with the café, the antique fixtures, that whole ribbon wall situation..." He gestured around, almost reverently. "The fresh flowers, the light in here—all of it. Do you mind if I look around?"

"Not at all," Liz said, setting down her upholstery tool. "Let me know if you have any questions."

For the next twenty minutes, the man explored the shop, occasionally taking photos with his phone. He examined Liz's furniture pieces closely, ran his hand along the reclaimed wood shelving, studied the seasonal display with its artfully displayed silk flowers and coastal accessories. He bought a coffee from Greg and sat at one of the small tables, pulling out a notebook and scribbling notes.

Finally, he approached where Liz and Greg were talking near the counter.

"I'm Jason Potter," he said, extending his hand. "I do a vlog about small businesses, unique spaces, places with character. I've covered spots all over the country."

"I'm Liz," she said, shaking his hand, "and this is my husband, Greg." Greg nodded in greeting. "Nice to meet you."

Jason paused. "Anyway, I'd love to feature this place. Your whole concept is exactly what my audience is interested in. Small-batch creativity, sustainable restoration, that intersection of commerce and craft."

"Feature us?" Liz asked. "Like, make a video?"

"Exactly," Jason said, his enthusiasm building. "I'm actually in Cape May shooting some content about small beach towns that are doing interesting things. Your place wasn't on my list. Honestly, I just needed a bathroom, but now that I've seen it, I have to include it. This is too good."

"What would it involve?" Greg asked.

"Just me filming for maybe an hour or two," Jason said. "I'll interview you both about your vision, show the space, watch you work, maybe some furniture restoration, making one of those incredible-looking sandwiches I saw someone eating. Then I edit it all together with music and post it."

"When?" Liz asked.

"I'm here for the week," Jason said. "How about Thursday? I'll come around two in the afternoon."

"Can we talk about it and let you know?" she asked.

"Absolutely," Jason said, pulling out a business card. "Here's my info. But honestly, I really hope you say yes. Your place has something special. Authenticity, heart, craft. That's rare these days."

After he left, Liz and Greg stood in the quiet café, looking at the business card.

"Well," Greg said finally. "That was unexpected."

"It could be good for business," Liz said.

"Couldn't hurt," Greg agreed.

They looked at each other.

"We should do it," they said in unison, then laughed.

The ocean breeze swept through the open windows of the beach house, catching the blue and white gingham curtains and sending them billowing into the room. The scent of salt water drifted in, mixing with the smell of the coffee she'd brewed. Margaret stood in the living room, her hands on her hips, surveying the space with satisfaction. After spending yesterday at Chris and Sarah's wedding and this morning cleaning, restocking, and freshening things up, everything was in place. The cream-colored sectional positioned perfectly to face the windows, the weathered wood side tables polished and gleaming, fresh throw pillows in coral and white that she'd just added to brighten the space.

"I think we're finally ready for summer," she said as Dave came down the stairs.

He grinned. "Really? I find that hard to believe."

She laughed, swatting his arm playfully. "Okay, mostly ready. Though I was thinking we could add a few more plants on the deck—"

"There it is," Dave said, his smile widening. "I knew it."

Margaret moved to the back door, looking out at the

private beach path that ran between their property and the neighbors'. It was a Sunday afternoon in May, and with Abby and Harper at a birthday party, she and Dave had the place to themselves for a few hours. The house sat on a quiet residential street in Cape May, tucked into a neighborhood of grand Victorians, summer cottages, and some year-round homes where kids played in the street and neighbors called out greetings from their porches. Unlike their West Cape May farmhouse with its sprawling acreage, this property was more modest. Just the house, a small yard, and access to the beach through the shared path.

"Should we walk down to the beach?" Dave asked, coming up behind her. "Break in that beach path properly?"

"Absolutely," Margaret said. "But first, I want to make sure everything's secure. I noticed earlier that the gate to the beach path wasn't latching properly."

They headed out the back door, past the small deck where Margaret had already arranged two Adirondack chairs. The property line was marked by a simple split-rail fence, with a wooden gate that opened onto the beach path.

Dave examined the latch, jiggling it a few times. "You're right, it's loose. I'll pick up a new one this week."

As they walked down the path toward the beach, cutting between houses and crossing the quiet side streets, the sound of the waves grew louder, mixing with the cries of seagulls overhead. The air smelled of salt and sun-warmed sand.

"I love it here," Margaret said softly as they emerged onto the beach. The afternoon sun sparkled on the water, and only a handful of people dotted the shoreline, including a few surfers waiting for waves, a family building a sandcastle, an older couple walking hand in hand near the water's edge.

"Me too," Dave agreed, slipping off his shoes. "It's so different from the farmhouse, but in a good way."

They strolled along the water's edge for a while, letting the cool waves lap at their feet. Margaret found herself thinking about how quickly their life had expanded. Just a year ago, they'd had only the farmhouse. Now they had this beach house too, and soon they'd be spending every weekend here once the girls were out of school.

"Look at that," Dave said, pointing up ahead. "Is that the couple from Christmas?"

Margaret squinted, recognizing the man and woman walking toward them. It was the family they'd met back in December during that surprise snowstorm, the ones whose kids had been sledding on the beach path.

"Mary! Rob!" Margaret called out, waving.

The couple's faces lit up with recognition. Rob was tall with an easy smile, while Mary had a friendly face and sun-lightened hair. They were both wearing shorts and T-shirts, looking comfortable in the beach environment.

"Margaret! Dave!" Mary said as they met. "We were wondering when you'd be back. Are you here for the weekend?"

"We're here for good," Margaret said. "Well, weekends anyway. We're getting the place ready for summer."

"That's wonderful," Rob said. "There's nothing quite like spending summer Saturdays and Sundays at the beach."

They chatted for a few minutes, catching up on the months since Christmas. Mary and Rob lived three houses down from Margaret and Dave, in a Cape Cod-style cottage with blue shutters. They'd been coming to Cape May for twenty years before finally buying a house five years ago.

"We're having a little gathering this afternoon, actually," Mary said. "Just a casual thing on our deck. Burgers on the grill, nothing fancy. You should come! There will be a few other neighbors there. It would be a great way for you to meet everyone. Well, most of them. The Mitchells can't make it, but you'll meet them soon."

Margaret glanced at Dave, who nodded. "We'd love to," she said.

"Perfect! Come by around four-thirty," Rob said. "Bring whatever you're drinking, and we'll provide the rest."

As they continued their walk, Margaret felt a flutter of excitement. "This is exactly what I was hoping for," she said. "Everyone's so welcoming."

"It's nice," Dave agreed, smiling as they turned back toward their house.

* * *

That afternoon, they headed down to Mary and Rob's house, Harper and Abby leading the way. Margaret carried a bottle of wine while Dave had a six-pack of craft beer. The sun was still bright and warm in the late-afternoon sky. Music drifted from the backyard, something bluesy and mellow, and Margaret could smell burgers on the grill.

"We can't stay too late," Margaret said to Dave quietly. "School tomorrow."

"I know," Dave said. "Just an hour or so."

"Back here!" Mary's voice called out when they knocked on the side gate.

The backyard was charming, with tiki torches flickering along the perimeter and a large wooden deck. About a dozen people were scattered around, some sitting at a picnic table, others standing by the grill, a few perched on the deck railing with drinks in hand. A group of kids were playing cornhole on the lawn, and Harper and Abby were immediately waved over by two girls around their age.

"Everyone, this is Margaret and Dave," Mary announced, gesturing to them. "They bought Howard's old place last fall."

"And that's Harper and Abby," Margaret added, pointing toward where the girls had already joined a group of kids on the lawn.

A chorus of friendly hellos greeted them. Rob appeared,

taking their drinks to add to the cooler before making introductions.

"This is Delores and Billy," he said, gesturing to a retired couple who looked to be in their early seventies. Billy had a distinguished head of silver hair and wore a Hawaiian shirt, while Delores wore a colorful sundress. "They've been here longer than anyone. Almost thirty years."

"Welcome to the neighborhood," Billy said, shaking their hands firmly. "Howard was good people. Glad to see the house going to someone who'll actually use it. Too many of these places sit empty most of the year now."

"That's our plan," Dave said. "We'll be here every weekend through the summer, and maybe more once the girls are out of school."

Rob guided them around the deck, continuing introductions. Gloria and Grant, a laid-back couple in their late forties whose teenage son and daughter were, according to Gloria, "somewhere causing trouble, as usual." Then there were Valerie and Artie, a couple in their early thirties who'd bought their house two years ago.

"We're still considered newbies," Artie said with a laugh. He was tall and athletic-looking, with sun-bleached hair and perfect teeth. "But the learning curve isn't too steep. Basically, you need to know the best spots for coffee, the tide schedule, and where to find good crab."

"Don't forget the most important thing," Valerie added, her dark curly hair falling into her eyes. "Friday night fish fries at Gil's Tavern. It's become our tradition."

"You should come this Friday," Gloria said, overhearing. "We all try to go together when we can. It's nothing fancy, but the food is great, and it's become kind of our unofficial neighborhood thing."

"That sounds great," Margaret said. "We'll be there."

As the evening progressed, Margaret found herself deep in conversation with Mary and Valerie about the best beaches for shelling, while Dave was pulled into a discussion with Billy about the best fishing spots along the coast. The sky deepened to dusky pink as the sun dropped toward the horizon, and someone turned up the music. Delores brought out a platter of homemade brownies, and more wine was opened.

"This is so different from our other neighborhood," Margaret told Mary as they sat on the deck steps, watching the last light fade from the sky. "In West Cape May, our neighbors are acres away. It took us forever to even meet them. But here, there's this instant sense of community."

Mary nodded. "That's the magic of this place. Everyone here loves the beach, loves this town, and there's just this natural camaraderie. We look out for each other."

Around seven-thirty, mindful of the school night ahead, they said their goodbyes. They returned to the beach house to grab their bags. Within twenty minutes, they were on the road back to West Cape May. It had been a perfect day, but the farmhouse and school awaited.

CHAPTER THREE

The distant crash of waves and the cries of seagulls filled the air as Donna unlocked the doors to Dale and Donna's Funnel Cakes, their shop on the Wildwood Boardwalk. It was the first week of the summer season, and excitement surged through her. They'd closed for the winter months, as they always did, and she'd spent weeks preparing for this reopening, deep cleaning, ordering supplies, hiring seasonal staff.

"Morning, boss!" Derek called out as he arrived for his first shift of the season. "Ready for another great summer?"

Donna smiled as she tied on her apron. "You know it. Let's make this our best year yet."

Annie arrived a few minutes later, pulling her hair back into a ponytail as she came through the door. "I couldn't wait to get here. Summer's officially here—I get to be down the shore again!" Her eyes lit up.

"That's the energy I like to see," Donna said with a laugh. "Let's get the fryers heating up."

By mid-morning, they had a decent crowd. Not quite the rush they'd hoped for, but steady enough. Donna stood behind the counter, greeting familiar faces and serving up their funnel cakes, including classic powdered sugar, strawberry topped, chocolate drizzled, and their popular cinnamon sugar. But something felt different. She couldn't quite put her finger on it at first.

Then she noticed the families walking past their window. Kids clutching extravagant desserts she'd never seen before, including tall cups filled with colorful layers, waffle cones shaped like bubbles, desserts that seemed to glow and sparkle. One teenager walked by with an ice cream sundae topped with lit sparklers, large churros popping out of it, and a mountain of whipped cream threatening to spill over the sides.

"Where are they getting those?" Derek asked, leaning forward to look out the window.

Donna shook her head. "I don't know. Must be something new."

As the late morning wore on, Donna decided to take a walk on the boards. It had transformed since last summer. Every few stores, there was a new dessert vendor, like a gourmet ice cream shop with seventy flavors, a water ice stand with exotic flavors like mango-chili and lychee, a cookie dough place where you could eat the dough raw, a custom donut stand with fancy toppings, a shop specializing in those bubble waffle cones she'd seen. They were used to competition on the boardwalk. It came with the territory, but something about this felt different.

Each shop had something in common: bright LED signs, Instagram-worthy presentations, lines of customers waiting to get in. She stopped in front of one place called "Magical Sweets Ice Cream Parlor" and observed through the window as they created showy sundaes with dry ice that created a smoky effect. Customers were taking videos on their phones before eating.

Donna headed back to her shop, her mind racing. Their classic funnel cakes suddenly felt plain. Old-fashioned. Boring, even. She hated thinking that way about something she'd worked so hard to build, but she couldn't deny what she was seeing.

The crowd was lighter than usual. A few people stopped in for funnel cakes, but nowhere near opening day last year. She could feel the difference. Donna found herself noticing as people walked past their window, heading toward one of the trendier dessert spots instead.

"Is it just me, or is this slower than we expected?" Derek asked as he wiped down the counter during a lull.

Donna didn't want to worry him. "It's only the first week. Things will pick up."

But she wasn't sure she believed it herself.

Around noon, Donna left the shop in Derek and Annie's hands and drove to Cape May to meet Dale at Donna's restaurant. He was starting lunch service when she walked into the kitchen.

"How's opening day?" he asked, pulling her in for a quick kiss.

Donna sighed. "Slower than expected. The boardwalk has changed, Dale. There are so many new dessert places, all of them flashy and trendy. We look boring in comparison."

Dale leaned against the host stand, sorting through the specials menu. "I'm sure it's just first-week nerves. Once word gets out that you're open again, people will come."

"Maybe," Donna said, though she wasn't convinced. "How about you? How's lunch going?"

"Good, actually. We just opened, but we're already filling up." He grabbed his keys from the hook. "Eduardo's got things covered in the back. Hey, I need to pick up some fresh seafood for tomorrow. There's a new supplier on the Wildwood boardwalk I want to check out. Want to ride with me?"

"Sure," Donna said.

Half an hour later, they were parking near the boardwalk. The afternoon crowd was building with families, teenagers, couples strolling hand in hand. The boardwalk was alive with music and the smells of a dozen different foods competing for attention.

Dale led the way toward the seafood supplier, which was located near Dale and Donna's Funnel Cakes. As they walked, Donna noticed Dale's pace slow. He stopped in front of a storefront she hadn't seen earlier that day.

"Sugar Rush Dessert Bar," Dale read aloud, studying the bright pink and blue neon signs. The place was massive, easily three times the size of their shop, with floor-to-ceiling windows that let you watch the entire operation. Inside, at least eight employees in matching bright-pink shirts moved with precision, creating elaborate desserts while dance music thumped from speakers.

"They must have just opened," Donna said. "I didn't see any customers when I walked by earlier."

But Dale wasn't listening. His face had gone pale as he gazed through the window. "That's interesting."

"What?" Donna asked, following his gaze.

At the center of the chaos inside stood a man with dark hair and an air of absolute confidence. He moved from station to station, adjusting technique here, demonstrating a flourish there. He was obviously in charge and clearly knew exactly what he was doing.

"That's Frank Larson," Dale said quietly, his voice tight. "My former sous chef."

Donna's eyes widened. She'd heard the name before. "The one who—"

"The one who left on bad terms. Yeah." Dale's jaw clenched. "He's running this place."

They stood there for a moment, peering through the window. Frank was demonstrating how to make a bubble waffle cone for a young couple, pouring batter onto the special gridded iron, folding it into a cone shape while still hot, adding mix-ins with theatrical flair. He filled it with soft serve ice cream, then topped it with whipped cream, edible glitter, and colorful toppings, then handed it over with a showman's smile.

"He's using everything I taught him," Dale said, his voice barely above a whisper. "Every technique about presentation, about creating an experience, about making it memorable. He worked under me for three years. I mentored him, taught him everything I knew about running a kitchen, about flavor profiles, about connecting with customers. And then he betrayed me. He tried to steal my recipes, poach my staff, open his own place using what I'd given him." Dale shook his head. "I fired him. He left angry, told me I was holding him back, that I'd regret it."

As if sensing he was being watched, Frank looked up toward the window. His eyes met Dale's, and for a moment, neither man moved. Then Frank smiled, slow and deliberate, and gave a small wave before turning back to his work.

Dale felt himself tense up. "He knew. He had to have known this is our spot. He did this intentionally."

Donna gently pulled Dale away from the window. "Come on. Let's go."

They moved in silence, stopping briefly at the shop so Donna could check in with Derek and Annie. When they got to the car and closed the doors, Dale sat gripping the steering wheel, eyes fixed on the road.

"He set up shop three stores down from us," Dale said. "Creating this flashy, trendy place that makes our classic funnel cakes look like ancient history. That smile he gave me? That was him saying, 'I won.'"

Donna didn't know what to say. She'd never seen Dale this rattled. "We don't know for certain—"

"I know Frank. This is exactly the kind of thing he'd do. He's been waiting for this chance. Waiting to prove that he's better than me, that firing him was my mistake." Dale started the engine. "And now he's set up right on top of us, stealing our customers with his bubble waffles and fancy sundaes and whatever other trendy nonsense he's selling."

As they drove back toward Cape May, Donna looked out the window. The excitement she'd felt that morning was gone, replaced by a gnawing worry. Their opening day had been disappointing. The boardwalk had become saturated with trendy dessert vendors. And now they had direct competition from someone who knew all of Dale's tricks, someone with a personal vendetta.

"What are we going to do?" she asked quietly.

Dale stared at the road ahead. "I don't know yet. But I'm not going to let Frank Larson steal our business. Not without a fight."

Donna nodded, but deep down, she wondered if fighting was the right answer, or if they were about to make things much worse.

* * *

Lisa sat at the small desk in her beach house rental, her laptop open to spreadsheets showing last month's sales figures for Current Culture, her online surf shop. The afternoon sun streamed through the window, warming her shoulders as she squinted at the numbers. Her eco-friendly surf wax, made from natural beeswax, tree resin, and coconut oil instead of petroleum-based ingredients, had been selling steadily, but the real stars lately were her organic cotton board shorts and her collaboration with a small surfboard shaper in California who used sustainable materials. She'd built Current Culture around a simple philosophy: surfers should protect the ocean that gave them so much joy. Every product was either biodegradable, made from recycled materials, or produced by manufacturers with strong environmental track records. It kept her margins tight, but she could sleep at night knowing she wasn't contributing to the plastic pollution choking the world's coastlines.

She'd just finished a video call with her warehouse manager about inventory. They were running low on the large-sized rash guards again when her phone buzzed, displaying a California number she didn't recognize.

"Hello?"

"Hi, is this Lisa? Owner of Current Culture?" A polished female voice came through the line.

Lisa minimized the spreadsheet on her screen. "That's me. Who's calling?"

"My name is Rebecca Nixon. I'm the VP of Brand Partnerships at Tidal Wave Sports. We're one of the largest surf and beach lifestyle companies in the country. Do you have a few minutes to talk?"

Lisa's heart skipped. She'd heard of Tidal Wave. They were massive, with stores up and down both coasts and a huge online presence. "Sure, of course."

"Great. So, I'll get right to it. We've been watching your brand for the past year, Lisa. Your Instagram following has grown exponentially, your products are getting rave reviews on surf forums, and our team is very impressed."

Lisa leaned back in her desk chair, trying to steady her breathing. "Thank you. That means a lot."

"We'd like to talk to you about a potential partnership. Actually, we're interested in discussing two options." Rebecca paused. "The first would be a licensing deal where we'd distribute your products nationally through our stores and website. You'd maintain ownership of your brand, and we'd handle all the logistics, marketing, and distribution. The second option, and I want you to hear me out on this, would be for Tidal Wave to acquire Current Culture outright."

The room suddenly felt smaller. Lisa stood and walked to the window, staring through the trees toward the glimpse of ocean beyond. "Acquire my company?"

"Yes. We're prepared to make a very generous offer. I can't get into specific numbers over the phone, but we're talking serious money, Lisa. Plus, you'd stay on as the creative director with a significant salary for at least three years. Your products would be in over three hundred stores within six months."

Lisa's mind raced. She thought about her beat-up VW bus in the driveway, the month-to-month rental she could barely afford even though her sales were growing. The truth was, every dollar Current Culture made went right back into the business, paying the factory upfront for new inventory, covering warehouse fees, funding her next product line. On paper, the business was doing well. In her personal bank account? She was living lean, constantly juggling factory orders and warehouse logistics, watching her cash flow like a hawk. One slow month, one delayed payment from a retailer, and she'd be scrambling. "I don't know what to say."

"You don't have to say anything right now. But I'd love to fly you out to our headquarters in San Diego next week. First-class ticket, nice hotel, the whole deal. You can meet our team, tour our facilities, and we can discuss both options in detail. No pressure, just a conversation. What do you say?"

Lisa closed her eyes, feeling the weight of the moment. The offer sounded incredible. She'd get national distribution, the kind of financial security she'd never had. But something in her gut twisted. She'd built Current Culture on principles that mattered to her, principles that didn't always align with corporate priorities. What would happen to that inside a massive company?

"Can I think about it for a day or two?"

"Of course. Take your time. I'll email you some preliminary information. My direct number will be in there if you have any questions. I really hope we can make this work, Lisa. We believe in what you're building."

After they hung up, Lisa sat frozen at her desk. Three hundred stores. National distribution. Life-changing money.

She thought about Nick, about Cape May, about the simple life she'd been trying to build here. Then she thought about the stack of unpaid invoices on her desk, the constant stress of making ends meet, the fear that one bad month could sink everything she'd worked for.

Her phone buzzed again. This time it was Nick.

"Hey, you," she answered, trying to sound normal.

"Hey." His voice sounded strained. "Can you come by the oyster farm? I need to talk to you about something."

Lisa heard the worry in his tone. "Is everything OK?"

"I don't know. Just… can you come?"

"I'll be there in twenty minutes."

When Lisa got to the oyster farm, she found Nick standing at the edge of one of his oyster beds, surveying the water with his hands on his hips. Two other workers were out on the water in waders, a younger guy and an older man with a weathered baseball cap. The afternoon sun glinted off the bay, and a few gulls circled overhead. Nick looked up when he heard her footsteps on the sand.

"Thanks for coming," he said, worry evident in his voice.

"What's going on?" Lisa asked, coming over to stand beside him.

Nick gestured to the water. "Something's wrong with this section. I noticed it yesterday, but I thought maybe I was overreacting. This morning, it's worse."

"What do you mean?"

He knelt down and lifted one of the mesh bags from the water. Inside, Lisa could see dozens of oysters. Nick opened the bag and pulled one out, examining it closely. "See how the shell is slightly open? That's not good. A healthy oyster keeps its shell shut tight when it's out of water." He dropped it back in and grabbed another. "Here's another one. And another."

She observed as he checked several more, his anxiety mounting with each one. "How many?"

"From what I can tell? At least thirty percent of these

oysters are showing signs of stress. Some are already dead." He stood up, running his hand through his hair. "Lisa, I've got about fifteen thousand oysters in this bed. If something's killing them, and I can't figure out what it is…"

"What happens?"

"I lose an entire season's crop. Maybe more if it spreads to the other areas." He looked at her, and she could see genuine fear in his eyes. "I've got restaurant contracts, obligations. The mortgage on the bay house. I can't afford to lose this."

"OK, so what do we do?" Lisa asked. "What could be causing it?"

"That's the thing. It could be a dozen different factors. Water quality, disease, predators, temperature changes, pollution. I need to test the water, check the salinity, look for signs of parasites or disease. I need to call a marine biologist I know at Rutgers and the state aquaculture office."

"How long will that take?"

"A few days for the water tests. Maybe a week to get someone out here to examine the oysters themselves. Meanwhile, I've got to check my other three beds every single day, sometimes twice a day. If this spreads…" He trailed off, shaking his head.

They stood in silence for a moment, watching the water lap against the shore.

"I'm glad you called me," Lisa said.

Nick looked at her. "I just needed you to see what's happening, you know? Sometimes I feel like I'm going crazy."

"You're not crazy," Lisa said firmly. "This is serious."

Nick managed a small smile despite everything. "Thanks for coming out. It means a lot."

For the next hour, Nick showed her around his operation, explaining what he and his crew were dealing with. He explained how he measured water temperature and salinity. He walked her through the complex ecosystem of the bay, how everything was connected. He explained water quality, weather patterns, pollution from upstream, even the moon's influence on the tides. Lisa could see how much he cared about this place, how deeply the mystery of what was killing his oysters was eating at him.

The younger worker, Tommy, waded over with another bag of oysters. "This one's even worse. I'd say forty percent are showing stress." He nodded at Lisa. "Hey."

"Hey," Lisa said, her eyes on Nick as he examined the bag.

Nick grimaced as he checked the oysters. "When did you pull this?"

"Just now, from the northwest corner." Tommy took off his hat and wiped his forehead. "I don't like this, Nick."

The older man, Aaron, called over from where he was checking another section. "Water temp's normal. Salinity's good. Nothing's adding up."

"That's what's killing me," Nick muttered. "Everything should be fine."

"This is May," Nick said to Lisa, as much to explain to her as to process it himself. "Prime growing season. These oysters should be fattening up, getting ready for summer harvest. Instead, they're dying, and I don't know why." He pulled up another bag, his movements more agitated now. "I've been doing this for eight years. I know these waters. I know my oysters. This doesn't make sense."

Aaron came closer. "You think it could be that algae bloom from last month? Sometimes those effects show up later."

"Maybe," Nick said, though he didn't sound convinced. "The water tests will tell us more."

They were checking the second bed when Tommy suddenly stopped, fixated on something in the water near the marker buoys.

"What?" Lisa asked.

He moved closer, reached down, and brought up something metallic. It was a small cage, the kind used for catching crabs. "Nick! Come look at this."

Nick sloshed over, his eyes narrowing when he saw what Tommy was holding. "This shouldn't be here."

"Maybe it just drifted in?" Lisa asked.

Nick shook his head, examining it more closely. "No, look—it's been placed deliberately. There's fresh bait in it." He stood up, scanning the area with new eyes. "Aaron, Tommy—check around the marker buoys. Look for more of these."

Over the next twenty minutes, the three of them found four more traps, all placed strategically around Nick's oysters. Nick's unease deepened with each discovery. Aaron shook his head. "This is intentional. Someone's messing with us."

"Who would do that?" Tommy asked, looking genuinely confused.

Nick examined the traps, his jaw tight. "These aren't just random. They're placed to disrupt the oysters, maybe even to poach them." He started gathering them, his movements deliberate. "Between the dying oysters and now this? Someone doesn't want me to succeed here."

Tommy looked at Lisa, then back at Nick. "What do we do?"

"I'm calling the marine police," Nick said. "This is illegal. You can't just place traps on someone else's lease area." He took out his phone, then looked at his workers. "Aaron, Tommy—can you two finish checking bed three? I need to make some calls."

"You got it," Aaron said. "Come on, Tommy."

As the two men waded off to check the remaining area, Nick made his calls, starting with the marine police, then to his insurance company, then to the marine biologist. Aaron and Tommy returned, both looking grim.

"That bed's showing signs too," Aaron said quietly. "Not as bad as the first one, but it's starting."

Nick closed his eyes for a moment, then nodded. "Alright. Thanks, guys. Head on home. We'll regroup tomorrow morning."

As they stood there, Lisa thought about the phone call from Tidal Wave, about the decision she still had to make. She glanced at Nick looking out at the water, worry etched across his face as he thought about his dying oysters and whoever was sabotaging his farm. Now didn't feel like the right time to bring up her own crossroads. That email was sitting in her inbox, waiting. A decision that could change everything for her. But it could wait another day.

CHAPTER FOUR

The humidity hit Sarah the moment they stepped out of Louis Armstrong International Airport. It was like walking into a warm, wet blanket, the kind of thick Louisiana air that made her dress cling to her back before they'd even reached the curb. Chris was beside her, already loosening his collar, his carry-on slung over one shoulder.

"Welcome to New Orleans," he said, beaming despite the sweat already forming at his temples.

"It's like breathing soup," Sarah said, but she felt a smile spread across her face. They were here. Actually here. On their honeymoon.

The past few days since the wedding had been a blur of thank-you notes and leftover cake, packing and repacking, and approximately seventeen conversations about whether they'd remembered to turn off the coffee maker. But now they were standing in New Orleans, married, and about to spend a week eating their way through the French Quarter.

Their cab driver, James, talked with his hands more than he used the steering wheel. He picked them up in a car with no air conditioning. The windows were down, but it didn't help. The air coming in was just more hot air, and James seemed completely unbothered by it, his Hawaiian shirt unbuttoned halfway down his chest, gold chains glinting in the sun.

"You want the real New Orleans experience?" he shouted over the sound of traffic, taking a turn so sharp that Sarah grabbed Chris's arm and Chris grabbed the door handle. "I'm gonna tell you where to eat! None of this tourist trap garbage!"

He swerved around a delivery truck, accelerating through a yellow light that was definitely more red than yellow. Sarah and Chris exchanged a look—the kind of look that said *we're going to die in New Orleans before we even check into our guest house.*

"Now Commander's Palace," James continued, completely oblivious to their terror as he narrowly missed a cyclist, "that's good food, but you gotta dress up. They make the men wear jackets. The turtle soup? Chef's kiss." He actually took both hands off the wheel to make the gesture, and Sarah felt her stomach drop.

James laughed, a big booming laugh that shook his whole body as he cut off a Mercedes and turned onto Burgundy Street on what might have been two wheels. "You two just get married or something? You got that honeymoon look."

"Yeah," Sarah managed, her knuckles white from gripping the seat. "A few days ago."

"Congratulations! You picked the right city! Romance, food, music—" He slammed on the brakes in front of their guest house, and both Sarah and Chris lurched forward. James twisted around to look at the building then let out a low whistle. "Oh man, you're staying here? This place is seriously haunted! Old shotgun house. They say a jazz musician died in one of the back rooms in the thirties. Still plays his trumpet at night." He grinned at their expressions. "Here you go! Thirty-six bucks!"

Sarah had never been so happy to see their destination in her life. They climbed out, legs shaky, clothes drenched in sweat from the nonexistent air conditioning.

"Have fun, lovebirds!" James called out the window before peeling away from the curb with a screech.

Sarah tilted her head back to take it in. It was a classic shotgun house, long and narrow, painted a faded purple with bright-green shutters. Wrought-iron details decorated the small front porch, and bougainvillea spilled over the fence. The sign by the gate read "Maison Beaumont Guest House" in elegant script. According to their booking confirmation, the owners lived in the front of the house, and the guest rooms were in the back. Two blocks from Frenchmen Street, three blocks from the French Quarter. After that cab ride, it looked like paradise.

Now, standing in the narrow front parlor that served as the reception area, Sarah watched as the desk clerk—a young woman with flawless winged eyeliner—typed on her laptop.

"Reservation is under Sarah Taylor," Sarah said. "Should be the honeymoon suite."

The clerk's smile brightened. "Congratulations! Let me just..." She frowned at the screen. "Hmm."

Chris felt a flutter of anxiety. "Is something wrong?" he asked.

"No, no, everything's fine. You're all checked in. It's just..." The clerk looked up, her expression apologetic. "We did have to make a small room change. There was a plumbing issue with the honeymoon suite. But we've upgraded you to one of our premium rooms at no extra charge."

"Oh," Chris said. "That's fine. Which room?"

"Room 3."

"Great," Chris said, taking the keys.

"You're going to love it. The room has beautiful original hardwood floors and French doors that open to the courtyard."

Room 3 was, Sarah had to admit, beautiful. High ceilings, exposed brick on one wall, a four-poster bed draped with gauzy white curtains. The French doors were open to a lush courtyard filled with banana trees, ferns, and flowering plants she couldn't name. Beyond their small patio, she could see the shared courtyard with its brick pathways and, tucked in one corner, a hot tub. The sounds of the neighborhood drifted in—car horns, snippets of jazz from somewhere nearby, the distant chatter of other guests.

Chris dropped his bag on the bed. "This is exactly what we needed."

Sarah walked to the French doors and looked out at the courtyard. The afternoon sun filtered through banana trees and cast dappled shadows on the brick pavers. This was perfect. A wonderful honeymoon in an incredible city with her perfect new husband.

Then a brass band started playing somewhere down the block, loud enough that she could hear every note clearly through the courtyard.

Chris came up beside her and gave her a playful nudge. "Come on. Let's go explore. I'm starving."

They'd researched restaurants for weeks, creating a shared note on Chris's phone with a list ranked by priority. Café Du Monde for beignets was number one, obviously. Commander's Palace for their twenty-five-cent martini lunch. A po'boy from somewhere authentic. Gumbo. Jambalaya. Pralines.

Now, walking through the French Quarter in the late-afternoon heat, Sarah felt like she was moving through a fever dream. Everything was bright and loud and slightly overwhelming. Street performers on every corner. The smell of fried food and garbage and flowers all mixed together. Tourists everywhere, cameras out, consulting maps on their phones.

They turned onto Decatur Street, heading toward the river, when Sarah heard it.

"Oh my GOD, Kevin, look at this! We have to get a picture!"

The voice was shrill, enthusiastic, and coming from directly behind them. Sarah turned to see a couple in matching "I Heart NOLA" T-shirts, the woman waving her phone at the man while he pulled out his own phone.

The woman—blond, probably in her late thirties, with an aggressive amount of jewelry—noticed Sarah watching and smiled brightly. "Are you guys here for the music?" she asked, gesturing vaguely toward Frenchmen Street.

"Yeah, among other things," Sarah said.

"Us too! Well, that and the food. We're on our honeymoon! Just got married last week in Boca Raton." Amber stuck out her hand, and Sarah noticed the enormous diamond ring and several chunky bracelets that jangled when she moved. "I'm Amber, this is Kevin."

They exchanged a glance. "We're on our honeymoon too," Sarah said. "Got married a few days ago."

"No way! Honeymoon twins!" Amber squealed. "We should totally do a double honeymoon photo! Kevin, get them in the shot!"

Before Sarah could protest, Amber had grabbed her arm and was positioning her next to Kevin while Chris stood there looking amused. Kevin held up his phone. "Say New Orleans!" and the flash went off.

"Perfect!" Amber said, checking the photo. "So where are you guys staying?"

"A guest house in the Marigny," Sarah said. "Maison Beaumont."

"Wait, Maison Beaumont?" Amber's eyes went wide. "That's where we're staying!"

Sarah felt something sink in her stomach. "You're staying at Maison Beaumont?"

"Yeah! Isn't that crazy?" Amber said. "We should totally hang out! Where are you guys eating tonight? We heard Brennan's is amazing, but we also want to try that place with the turtle soup. What's it called, Kevin?"

"Commander's Palace," Kevin said, consulting his own phone.

That was on their list. Sarah looked at Chris, who was trying very hard not to laugh.

"We're actually just going to play it by ear," Chris said smoothly. "See where the day takes us."

"Oh, spontaneous! I love that!" Amber said. "We're super planned out. Kevin made this whole spreadsheet." She showed them her phone, which displayed what appeared to be a color-coded itinerary with fifteen-minute increments.

Sarah stared at the spreadsheet. It was thorough. Intimidatingly thorough.

"Well," Sarah said, "we should probably—"

"Beignets!" Amber practically shouted. "Are you going to Café Du Monde? We're going right now! You should come!"

Chris glanced at Sarah, a silent question. She looked at Amber and Kevin, at their matching shirts and their obvious, uncomplicated enthusiasm. They seemed nice. Overwhelming, but nice.

"Sure," Sarah heard herself say. "Beignets sound great."

Café Du Monde was packed, every table filled with tourists wielding cameras and napkins, the air thick with powdered sugar. They found a table near the back, and Amber immediately started chatting with the neighboring diners.

"We're on our honeymoon! Just got married last week! You guys been here before? We heard the beignets are life-changing!"

The couple nodded politely and went back to their coffee.

Sarah bit her lip to keep from smiling. Next to her, Chris was doing the same thing. When the beignets arrived—hot, pillowy, and buried under an avalanche of powdered sugar—Amber insisted everyone wait while she took a photo, then she tried to get the neighboring couple to take a group shot of all four of them.

"It'll be so cute! Honeymoon memories!"

They bit into their beignets. Powdered sugar exploded everywhere, coating Sarah's face, her dress, the table, probably the people nearby. The beignet itself was heavenly—light, airy, still warm, with just enough resistance to make eating it feel like an accomplishment.

"Wow," Chris said, his face covered in white powder. "These are incredible."

"Right?" Amber said through a mouthful of beignet, somehow managing to look cute despite the sugar mustache. She turned to them again. "Aren't these amazing?"

The couple nodded and focused very intently on their own food.

After Café Du Monde, they managed to politely disentangle themselves from Amber and Kevin, promising to maybe meet up later, maybe tomorrow, definitely before the end of the trip.

"They're staying at our guest house," Sarah said as they walked.

"I know."

"They're going to all the same restaurants we are."

"Probably."

Sarah stopped walking. "Are you worried we're going to run into them everywhere?"

Chris thought about this. "Honestly? Yeah. A little." He laughed. "But it could be worse. They could be awful. They're just... enthusiastic."

"Very enthusiastic," Sarah agreed. She looked down at herself, still covered in powdered sugar. "I should probably clean up before we do anything else."

"Good idea," Chris said, brushing sugar off his own shirt. "Let's go back to the room, then we can explore before dinner."

They walked toward the Marigny, the streets gradually becoming quieter as they left the tourist-heavy Quarter behind. Back in their room, they both changed out of their powdered-sugar-covered clothes. Sarah put on a sundress and comfortable sandals. Chris switched to a clean shirt.

"Much better," Sarah said, checking herself in the mirror.

They headed back out into the afternoon heat, this time wandering through the Quarter at a more leisurely pace. Sarah bought a small watercolor of a French Quarter courtyard from an artist on Jackson Square. Chris found a vintage jazz poster in a dusty shop on Royal Street that he insisted they needed for the house.

They stopped at a voodoo shop where a woman with elaborate braids tried to sell them love potions and gris-gris bags. "For love," she said knowingly. Chris bought one, flashing a smile at Sarah's eye roll. In a bookstore that smelled like old paper and incense, Sarah found a first edition Faulkner that made her heart skip, but the price tag made her put it back.

As the afternoon stretched on, they wandered past more galleries and a shop selling Mardi Gras masks. Eventually, Chris checked his phone. "We should probably head back and get ready for dinner."

Back in their room, Chris headed straight for the shower while Sarah tried to brush the humidity out of her hair. She changed into a nicer dress for GW Fins, and was putting on earrings when she heard it. A low, mournful note, like someone playing a trumpet in a distant room.

She froze. "Chris?"

"Yeah?"

"Do you hear that?"

He came out of the bathroom, listening. The trumpet played another note, then another, building into something that might have been a melody if the person playing knew what they were doing.

"That's coming from outside," Chris said, walking to the French doors. He looked out at the courtyard then toward the street. "Yeah. Street performer."

"Good," Sarah said.

Chris raised an eyebrow. "You were totally worried it was a ghost."

She threw a pillow at him.

They'd made reservations at GW Fins for dinner, a seafood place Chris had read about that printed a new menu every day based on what was fresh.

The restaurant was in a renovated turn-of-the-century warehouse, with high ceilings and large windows overlooking the French Quarter. It was upscale but not stuffy, the kind of place where serious foodies came for the catch of the day. Their waiter walked them through the menu, explaining where each fish had come from and how it would be prepared.

Chris ordered the lobster dumplings to start, then wood-grilled fish. Sarah got the "Scalibut"—half scallop, half halibut—seared and served with a lemon butter sauce. They shared a bottle of white wine that the sommelier recommended.

"To us," Chris said, raising his glass.

"To us," Sarah echoed. "And to street performers and way too much powdered sugar."

They clinked glasses. The wine was exquisite. The food, when it arrived, was even better. The Scalibut was beautifully seared, the texture somehow both firm and delicate. The lobster dumplings were rich and buttery, and Chris's wood-grilled fish came with a crispy skin that crackled when he cut into it.

Chris tried to describe the wood-grilled fish and gave up halfway through, just gesturing at his plate and making appreciative noises.

"I know," Sarah said, because she did. Her Scalibut was transcendent.

They were halfway through dessert—salty malty ice cream pie that was somehow both sophisticated and nostalgic—when she saw them.

Amber and Kevin. Heading toward the bar. Amber spotted them immediately and changed course.

"You guys!" Amber veered over, her voice carrying across the dining room. Several other diners looked up. "We couldn't get into Brennan's, so we came here instead! We're on the waiting list. The host said it might be two hours, but Kevin read that if you come after nine you can usually get seated faster." She leaned over their table, inspecting their dessert. "What is that? It looks fantastic!"

"Salty malty ice cream pie," Chris said.

"Kevin! We have to get that!" Amber said at full volume. She picked up the dessert menu from a nearby empty table. "Where is it? I don't see it. Is it a special?"

Kevin was already asking their waiter about it, even though he wasn't their waiter.

"The lobster dumplings were incredible," Chris said, apparently deciding to embrace the situation. "You should definitely get them."

"Adding it to the list!" Amber said, then let out a loud laugh that made several nearby diners turn and look. She didn't seem to notice. "Sorry, we're just so excited! This is our first time here and everyone said we had to try this place!" She was talking to the entire section now, not just Sarah and Chris.

Nearby diners exchanged an annoyed glance.

After finally extracting themselves from Amber and Kevin, Sarah and Chris stepped out onto the street. The night was warm, and they decided to walk back through the Quarter instead of going straight to the guest house. Music spilled out of every doorway on Frenchmen Street. Brass bands, blues guitar, a woman singing something that made Sarah's chest ache even though she couldn't make out the words.

"Should we?" Chris asked, gesturing toward a club with a hand-painted sign that read "The Spotted Cat."

Inside, it was packed. Bodies pressed together, everyone swaying to a small jazz band on a tiny stage. The trumpet player wore suspenders and a bowler hat. The upright bass player had a gray beard down to his chest. The woman on clarinet couldn't have been more than twenty-five, and she played like she'd been doing it for fifty years.

They squeezed into a spot near the back. Chris ordered

beers from a bartender who looked like he'd been serving drinks since before jazz had a name. The music was loud, joyful, the kind of thing that made you want to dance even if you'd never danced in your life.

"This place is unbelievable," Sarah said, leaning close to Chris's ear so he could hear her.

He nodded, grinning. His foot was already tapping.

A man next to them—older, wearing a suit despite the heat—suddenly let out a whoop and started dancing. Not carefully, not with any regard for the people around him. He spun, arms out, nearly knocking Sarah's beer out of her hand.

"Sorry, darlin'!" he shouted over the music, not sounding sorry at all. "Can't help it! This music gets in your bones!"

He kept dancing, and soon other people joined him. The space that had seemed packed before somehow made room for a dozen people to move. Sarah found herself pulled into it, Chris's hand in hers, both of them laughing as they tried to keep up with the rhythm.

The trumpet player started a solo that built and built, and the crowd went wild. Someone handed Sarah a tambourine. She had no idea where it came from or who gave it to her, but suddenly she was shaking it, and Chris was clapping, and the whole room felt like one big, chaotic celebration of being alive.

When the song ended, everyone applauded and whooped. The trumpet player took off his hat and bowed. The bass player immediately started the next song without pause, and the whole thing began again.

They stayed for three more songs before the heat and the beer and the sheer energy of the room became too much. Outside, the street felt cool by comparison, even though it was probably still eighty degrees.

"That was incredible," Sarah said. Her hair was damp with sweat, and she was pretty sure her dress was completely wrinkled, but she didn't care.

"Best fifteen dollars I've ever spent," Chris said, referring to the cover charge.

They walked the two blocks back to Maison Beaumont slowly, taking in the sounds of the neighborhood. Someone was playing piano in a house with open windows. A group of people sat on a stoop, passing around what might have been a bottle of whiskey. A cat watched them from a shadowy garden.

Back at the guest house, the courtyard was quiet. The hot tub in the corner was lit up, bubbles rolling across the surface.

"We have champagne," Chris said, remembering the split of champagne the front desk had left in their room as a honeymoon gift.

"Are you thinking what I'm thinking?" Sarah asked.

Ten minutes later, they were both in the hot tub, the champagne bottle sitting on the edge. Sarah had changed into her bathing suit. Chris had put on swim trunks. The water was just right, hot but not too hot, the bubbles working magic on Sarah's tired feet.

"This is bliss," she said, taking a sip of champagne. The bubbles tickled her nose. Above them, the sky was hazy with light pollution from the city, but she could still make out a few stars.

"Better than bliss," Chris said. He was stretched out across from her, his head back, eyes closed. "I don't want to move for the rest of the night."

They sat in comfortable silence for a while, the sounds of the city floating over the courtyard walls. Someone laughed in the distance. A car horn honked. Music from Frenchmen Street carried on the breeze, faint but unmistakable.

Sarah looked into their room. The lamps inside glowed softly, making everything look soft and inviting. She was just about to suggest they get out and go to bed when the lights flickered.

Not dramatically. Just a quick flutter, like someone had jiggled a switch.

"Did you see that?" she asked.

Chris opened his eyes, following her gaze. "See what?"

"The lights. They flickered."

He looked at the room. The lights were steady now, completely normal. "Old building," he said with a shrug. "Probably just the wiring."

"Right," Sarah said. "Old building."

She took another sip of champagne and settled deeper into the hot tub. The lights flickered again, so quickly she almost missed it. This time, she didn't say anything. Old wiring, she told herself. That's all it was.

But somewhere in the back of her mind, she could hear James's voice from that afternoon: Jazz musician died there in the thirties. Still plays his trumpet at night.

Tourist talk, she thought firmly. Just tourist talk.

Sarah took a long sip of champagne. This was going to be a very interesting honeymoon.

CHAPTER FIVE

Judy fastened her seatbelt as Bob pulled out of the driveway. It was a gorgeous May morning, the kind where the air felt fresh but the sun promised warmth. They'd gotten into the habit of taking walks around Lake Lily a few times a week, and today seemed perfect for it.

"Perfect day for a walk," Bob said, turning onto Sunset Boulevard.

"It really is," Judy agreed, gazing out the window. As they approached Seagrove Ave., she glanced to her left and caught sight of the lighthouse. The red brick tower rose majestically in the distance. "I was reading something interesting in one of those magazines at the bookstore."

"Oh yeah? What's that?"

"It was about exercises for people our age. Apparently, climbing stairs is one of the best things you can do. Better than just walking on flat ground because it builds muscle, not just cardio." She kept her eyes on the lighthouse as they passed. "Gets your heart rate up more efficiently."

Bob nodded slowly. "Makes sense. I've definitely felt it when we've had to climb stairs anywhere."

Judy turned to him. "So I was thinking... what if instead of walking around the lake today, we climbed the Cape May Lighthouse?"

Bob glanced over at her, eyebrows raised. "The lighthouse? Right now?"

"Why not? It's a beautiful day for it, and when was the last time you actually climbed it? I bet it's been a while."

Bob rubbed the back of his neck with one hand, keeping the other on the wheel. "You're not wrong. I think it's been a few years at least."

"Exactly!" Judy said, her enthusiasm building. "Great views from the top, and it'll definitely give us a better workout than our usual walk. Plus, we can always do Lake Lily another day."

Bob was quiet for a moment, and Judy could tell he was considering it.

"All right," he said finally, turning onto Lighthouse Ave. "Let's give it a try. We'll save the lake for another day."

Judy smiled and settled back in her seat. "We'll take it slow."

A few minutes later, they pulled into the parking lot at Cape May Point State Park. The lot was nearly empty, with just a couple of other cars scattered about.

They walked along the path toward the lighthouse, the red brick and white trim of the tower rising against the blue sky ahead of them. Bob had to admit, even though he'd seen it many times over the years, there was something impressive about the structure. The lighthouse had been standing there since 1859, surviving countless storms and harsh coastal weather. He'd read somewhere that the walls at the bottom were almost four feet thick, built sturdy enough to handle the worst weather nature could throw at it.

"You know," Bob said as they approached the entrance, "this is the third lighthouse they built here. The first two are underwater now because of erosion."

Judy glanced at him. "I didn't know that. Where'd you learn it?"

"Read it somewhere. The first one was built in 1823, but the ocean started surrounding it at high tide, so they built another one in 1847. Same thing happened to that one eventually."

"Well, let's hope this one stays put," Judy said with a smile.

They paid their admission at the Oil House visitor center, where a cheerful young woman handed them brochures and reminded them to take their time on the climb.

"There are six landings with benches," she said. "Feel free to rest whenever you need to. And the interpretive panels on each level tell you about the lighthouse's history."

Bob thanked her, and they made their way to the base of the tower. The cast iron spiral staircase wound upward, disappearing into shadows above. The metal gridwork was open, allowing views down through the steps, something Bob tried not to think too hard about.

"Ready?" Judy asked, placing her hand on the railing.

"As I'll ever be."

They started climbing. The first twenty steps weren't bad. Bob's legs felt strong, and he found a rhythm quickly. But by the time they reached the first landing, he could feel his heart working harder.

"Okay," he said, pausing to catch his breath. "I see what you mean about the heart rate."

Judy laughed, only slightly winded. "And we've barely started."

Bob read the interpretive panel on the first landing aloud while giving his legs a moment to recover. It was something about the original lamps and the massive Fresnel lens that had once been housed at the top.

They climbed steadily, stopping at each landing to rest and read the interpretive panels. One described the daily life of lighthouse keepers and their families who'd lived at the station. Harry Palmer, a keeper in the 1920s and 30s, had won awards for maintaining beautiful gardens, even growing prize-winning hydrangeas and a half-acre vegetable garden. Bob smiled at the image of a lighthouse keeper tending pole beans and tomatoes between his shifts.

By the third landing, Bob could feel the effort in his legs. But there was something satisfying about pushing through, about proving to himself that he could still do something physically challenging. He thought about the lighthouse keepers who'd climbed these stairs every day, multiple times a day, to tend the light, trim the wicks, clean the lens. They'd done it in all weather, day and night, year after year.

"Three more landings," Judy said. "We're halfway there."

They continued upward, the spiral seeming to wind on forever. At one landing, they read about the lighthouse's role during World War II, when it had gone dark to avoid guiding enemy submarines.

"I can see the top," Judy said, looking up through the spiral of stairs above them.

They kept climbing. A few landings later, Judy's eyes were bright with anticipation. "Last push," she said.

And then, suddenly, they were at the gallery level, stepping out onto the watch gallery that circled the top of the lighthouse.

The view took their breath away.

Below them, Cape May Point State Park stretched out in a patchwork of walking trails, trees lush with fresh spring foliage, and the distinctive concrete remains of Battery 223 on the beach. The World War II bunker now sat partially in the surf, a victim of coastal erosion. Beyond the park, he could see Cape May spreading to the north, the Victorian rooftops and tree-lined streets creating a postcard-perfect scene. To the east, the Atlantic Ocean glittered in the morning sun, the water a deep blue-green that seemed to go on forever.

"Look," Judy said, pointing south.

Bob followed her gaze. Along the shoreline, a flock of shorebirds darted along the waterline. He thought they might be sanderlings. Their small bodies moved in perfect synchronization as they chased the retreating waves. They moved as one organism, banking left, then right, their white undersides flashing in the sunlight.

"That's incredible," Bob said softly.

"I know." Judy leaned on the railing, taking in the view. "I'm glad we did this."

To the west, Bob could just make out Cape Henlopen, Delaware, across the mouth of Delaware Bay, exactly as the brochure had promised on a clear day. Several boats dotted the water. Fishing boats were heading out for the day, maybe some early-season recreational vessels making the most of the pleasant weather.

Bob turned his attention back to the beach below, his gaze settling on Battery 223. The massive concrete bunker sat at the edge of the surf, its weathered walls stark against the sand. He'd seen it countless times over the years, but from up here, the whole structure was laid out below them. Every crack in the concrete, the exposed rebar, the way the waves lapped at its base.

"That thing always looks like it's about to wash into the ocean," Judy said, following his gaze.

"One of these days it probably will," Bob agreed.

He was about to look away when movement caught his eye. A figure in dark clothing was making their way around the far side of the bunker. It was the side facing away from the main beach and parking lot.

"Judy."

"Hmm?"

"Look at the bunker. Someone's there."

Judy leaned forward, squinting. "I see them. Probably just someone exploring. People walk around it all the time."

But Bob kept watching. The figure wasn't walking around the bunker casually like a tourist. They were moving purposefully, checking over their shoulder, then stopping at the seaward side of the bunker. It was the side facing away from the main beach.

"They're doing something at the bunker," Bob said quietly.

Judy followed his gaze. "Looks like they're checking something out."

Bob didn't respond, his eyes fixed on the figure below. The figure crouched down, seemed to fidget with something. Maybe examining the concrete or the exposed pilings. Then they slipped out of view behind the bunker's bulk.

Bob glanced at his watch. 8:30 AM. About a minute later, the person came back into view, and this time Bob could see they were carrying something. A small bag or pack. As they stepped back into the open, a puff of dust or debris seemed to follow them, as if they'd disturbed something settled in the concrete's shadows.

The figure paused, pulled out binoculars, and scanned the water. Bob followed their line of sight and spotted it. A small boat, maybe a fishing boat, sitting relatively still about a quarter mile offshore.

"What are they looking at?" Judy asked.

"There's a boat out there."

The person lowered the binoculars then moved quickly north along the beach past the bunker to a spot near some dunes. They set down the bag, pulled out what looked like a small folding shovel, and started digging.

"They came prepared," Bob said softly.

The digging was quick, efficient. Within two minutes, they'd created a hole, placed the bag inside, and covered it back up. But they didn't stop there. They arranged several pieces of driftwood in what looked like a deliberate pattern, almost like an arrow or marker pointing at an angle.

Then the person stood, brushed sand from their dark pants, picked up the folding shovel, and walked briskly north along the beach—not back toward the parking lot, but in the opposite direction, staying close to the dunes.

"Did they just—" Judy started.

"Bury whatever they were carrying," Bob finished. "And mark the spot."

Bob tried to fix the location in his mind. A short distance north of the bunker, near a patch of beach grass that was slightly taller than the rest, marked now by the deliberate arrangement of driftwood.

A few other visitors had joined them on the watch gallery now. An older couple immediately began taking photos, and a young family with two kids pressed their faces against the railing, delighted by the height. Bob and Judy shifted to make room, moving a few feet around the circular platform.

Bob looked back toward the beach, but from this new angle he couldn't see the spot where the person had been digging. He could see the bunker though, sitting solid and mysterious.

Bob and Judy exchanged glances.

"I think we should make this our thing," Judy said, her voice thoughtful. "Our morning routine. Climb the lighthouse, see what we can see from up here."

Bob nodded, his eyes still on Battery 223 below. "You know what? I think you're onto something. Who knows what else we might spot from up here?"

They stayed at the top for another ten minutes, pointing out other sights to each other. A container ship far out on the horizon, a lone kayaker paddling close to shore, a hawk circling above the park. Bob kept glancing back at the beach near the bunker, trying to memorize exactly where that person had been digging. The 360-degree view offered something new with every turn, but his mind kept returning to what they'd witnessed.

Finally, Judy checked her watch. "We should probably head back down."

They made their way back down the spiral staircase, taking it slowly. The sun had climbed higher, warming the May air.

They walked slowly back to the car, both of them quiet, still processing the experience.

As they drove home, Bob found himself thinking about the view from the top, about the bunker on the beach, about the figure moving with such purpose. There was something deliberate about what they'd seen—too deliberate to be innocent curiosity.

* * *

Margaret and Dave arrived at the beach house mid-morning. The girls were in school, and they'd both wrapped up work for the day early, deciding to drive over from West Cape May to drop off some supplies. A new coffee maker, some books for the shelves Dave was building, a few other odds and ends.

Margaret was carrying bags in from the car when she noticed two college-aged guys walking through the backyard carrying beach chairs and a cooler. They moved with such ease and familiarity, as if they had every right to be there. She watched them push through the gate and disappear down the path between the houses.

Inside, she found Dave unpacking boxes in the living room.

"There were some people cutting through the yard just now," she said. "I didn't recognize them."

Dave looked up from the bookshelf pieces he was sorting. "Huh. That's weird. Maybe friends of one of the neighbors?"

"Maybe," Margaret said, but something about it had felt off.

But it kept happening throughout the day.

Margaret was in the kitchen, setting up the new coffee maker, when she heard voices in the backyard again. She glanced out the window and saw another group of strangers. Four or five people laden with bags, towels, and a large umbrella were walking through their yard toward the gate that led to the shared beach path.

"Dave," she called.

He came in from the living room. "What's up?"

"There are more people cutting through." She gestured out the window. "I don't recognize them either."

Dave moved to stand beside her, watching as the group made their way across the lawn toward the gate. They were laughing and talking loudly, acting like they had every right to be there.

"Huh. That's the second group today."

"Yeah," Margaret said.

They watched the strangers push through the gate and disappear down the path between the houses. Margaret felt a small knot of irritation forming in her chest, but she wasn't quite sure what to do about it.

"Should we say something?" she asked.

Dave shrugged, already turning back toward the living room. "I don't know. I mean, it's our property, but... maybe that's just how things work around here? Maybe everyone trespasses?"

"Maybe," Margaret said.

By late afternoon, several more groups had cut through their yard. When Dave suggested they pack up and head back, Margaret agreed. But as they were loading the car, Mary called out from her yard.

"Hey, neighbors!" she called, waving. "What are you two up to tonight?"

"Heading back to West Cape May," Dave said. "Just dropped some stuff off."

"Oh no, you should stay! We're doing an impromptu movie night in our backyard. Rob set up the projector screen, and we're showing *Jaws* because, you know, beach town tradition." She grinned. "Nothing fancy, just neighbors hanging out. You should join us!"

Margaret glanced at Dave. They had nothing pressing back home, and Abby and Harper would be thrilled. A rare late night on a school night, but it would be worth it. "We'd have to go back and pick up the girls first," she said. "But we could come back."

Dave hesitated, and she could see something flicker across his face—reluctance, maybe? But then he smiled. "Sure, why not?"

"Perfect!" Mary said. "Come by around eight. Bring blankets and whatever you want to drink."

* * *

As the sun began to set, they walked down to Mary and Rob's house, the girls ahead of them, already texting friends. The backyard had been transformed into an outdoor theater. A large white sheet hung between two trees, folding chairs and blankets spread across the lawn, and string lights creating a warm glow overhead.

"Margaret! Dave!" Rob called from where he was adjusting the projector. "Grab a spot wherever. We've got popcorn, s'mores fixings, the works."

Billy and Delores were already settled in lawn chairs near the front, and Valerie and Artie were spreading a large quilt on the grass. Gloria and Grant arrived moments later with their teenagers, who immediately claimed spots near Harper and Abby.

"This is amazing," Margaret said to Mary, who was setting out bowls of candy.

"It's become kind of a thing," Mary said. "Every few weeks in the warmer months, someone hosts. Last month, Gloria did *The Sandlot*. Before that, Artie and Valerie screened *Finding Nemo* for the kids."

As the sky darkened, more neighbors arrived. Margaret counted at least twenty people. A mix of families, couples, and a few solo attendees she hadn't met yet. The atmosphere was easy and warm, with kids running around catching fireflies, older teens clustered together laughing and scrolling through their phones, while the adults chatted and passed around bottles of wine.

"How are things going with the house?" Delores asked, settling into a chair beside Margaret.

"We love it here," Margaret said, and she meant it. "We're just figuring out the logistics of two places. Here and our home in West Cape May."

"That's always the challenge with a second home," Delores said knowingly. "Billy and I used to have a place upstate. We'd drive ourselves crazy trying to maintain two properties, two sets of friends, two lives. Eventually, we sold the upstate place and committed full-time to Cape May."

Margaret nodded, tucking that observation away. She glanced over at Dave, who was laughing at something Rob had said, and felt a small tug of concern. He'd been quieter than usual this afternoon.

The movie started, and everyone settled in. The adults called out favorite lines during the slower moments, and conversations continued in low murmurs.

Dave came over and sat down on the blanket beside Margaret, and Valerie shifted her chair closer. "So I've been meaning to ask," Valerie said during a particularly tense scene. "Have you guys had any issues with beach traffic through your yard?"

Margaret and Dave exchanged glances. "Actually, yes," Margaret admitted. "We had several groups walking through our yard today. We weren't sure if we should say something or if that's just... normal around here?"

"Oh no, that's the worst," Gloria said, overhearing. "It happens to everyone on this block. People see the path and assume it's public access."

"We had a group last summer who were cutting through multiple times a day," Artie added. "When we finally said something, the guy got in my face about how the beach belongs to everyone."

"What did you do?" Dave asked.

"Called the police, eventually," Artie said. "When we asked them to leave, the guy started yelling about public beach access and property rights. It was a whole thing."

Billy turned around in his chair. "You need to put up a sign. Clear, direct: 'Private Property. Beach Access for Residents Only.' And if people still don't listen, don't hesitate to call the cops. They're used to it."

"I just hate being that person," Margaret said. "We're new to the neighborhood, and I don't want to start off as the people who are always complaining."

"You're not complaining," Mary said firmly. "You're setting boundaries. Trust me, everyone here has dealt with it. The town gets so packed in the summer that people get entitled. They think because they paid for parking or rented a house, they can go wherever they want."

"It's different from our place in West Cape May," Dave said. "There, we're on acres of land. Here..." He trailed off, looking back at the movie screen, but Margaret could sense his discomfort.

The movie continued, and eventually the conversation shifted back to the on-screen action. But Margaret found herself watching Dave more than the movie. He laughed in the right places, made small talk with the neighbors, but there was something distant in his expression.

When the movie ended and they were gathering their things, she touched his arm. "You okay?"

"Yeah, of course," he said, though something seemed off. "Just tired."

They said their goodbyes and walked back to the beach house to grab their things. The girls chattered about the movie, reenacting their favorite scenes, while Margaret and Dave walked in companionable silence.

Inside, while the girls gathered their backpacks, Margaret found Dave standing at the back window, looking out at the dark yard.

"What are you thinking about?" she asked, joining him at the window.

He was silent for a moment. "I was just thinking about our house. Our main house in West Cape May. We haven't been there much lately. Just weeknights, really, and even then we're usually exhausted from work."

Margaret nodded, not sure what to say.

"And I love this place, I really do," he continued. "The neighbors are great, the beach is amazing, the girls are having a blast. It's just..."

"What?"

"I don't know. This is... different than I expected, I guess. My place on the bay was quiet—just me, and Chris and Sarah next door. But this..." He gestured vaguely toward where they'd come from. "All these neighbors, the constant activity. It's a lot —not bad, just a lot. And I almost feel like we're cheating on our house in West Cape May. Does that sound crazy?"

Margaret couldn't help but smile. "A little. But I get it."

CHAPTER SIX

Donna arrived at Dale and Donna's Funnel Cakes at six-thirty in the morning to find the lights already on.

She unlocked the door and found her husband hunched over the prep counter, surrounded by what could only be described as funnel cake carnage. Batter dripped down the sides of mixing bowls. Powdered sugar dusted every surface like snow. In the center of it all sat three elaborate creations that looked less like funnel cakes and more like abstract art installations.

"Dale?" Donna asked carefully. "How long have you been here?"

He looked up, eyes bleary but gleaming with manic energy. "I cracked it, Donna. Look at this." He pointed to the nearest creation, a funnel cake twisted into a perfect golden tower, the layers held together with salted caramel that caught the light like amber, topped with honey lavender ice cream, fresh berries, and a sparkler stuck in the top. "The Funnel Cake Spectacular. It's got height, drama, actual flavor complexity, and that Instagram-worthy factor Frank's place has."

Donna stared at the leaning tower of fried dough. She'd

woken up around three in the morning to find his side of the bed empty, but she'd assumed he'd fallen asleep on the couch. "Have you been here since four?"

"A little before, yeah." He grabbed another creation. This one was actually shaped like an elegant swan, the funnel cake piped and shaped with surprising precision, its hollow body filled with vanilla pastry cream. "And this is the Funnel Cake Fantasy. We fill it with the cream, dust it with cinnamon and cardamom, add the dry ice effect for smoke, and serve it with warm cherry compote on the side—"

"Dale, you have lunch service at the restaurant today."

"I know, I know. But listen." He pulled out his phone and showed her a video of Sugar Rush Dessert Bar. "Frank posted this last night. He's doing a 'Bubble Waffle Challenge'. If you can eat their largest sundae in under ten minutes, it's free. It already has ten thousand views."

Donna gently took the phone from his hands. "So your solution is to... build funnel cake skyscrapers?"

"Not just that." Dale moved to the counter, where another batch of batter waited. "I'm working on a funnel cake with pockets of liquid nitrogen ice cream. It flash-freezes on contact, creates this amazing texture contrast. And a s'mores version with toasted Italian meringue, house-made graham cracker crumble. Plus I'm thinking we could do a build-your-own bar with artisan toppings: real fruit coulis, tempered chocolate, bourbon caramel, fresh whipped cream with different flavor infusions—"

"Dale—"

"I called that specialty food supplier in Atlantic City. They can get us Tahitian vanilla beans, Valrhona chocolate, edible flowers that actually taste good, not just the decorative ones—"

"Dale!"

He stopped mid-sentence, looking at her with those exhausted, determined eyes.

Donna took a breath. "You need sleep."

"I don't need sleep. I need to show Frank Larson that he can't just waltz onto our boardwalk and—"

"Go home. Shower. Get some actual rest. And then go run your restaurant."

Dale crossed his arms. "So you're just going to let him win?"

"I'm not letting anyone win. I'm trying to keep my husband from having a breakdown over funnel cakes." She gestured at the chaos around them. "Look at this place. You've been here for six hours making... what are these, exactly?"

"Innovations," Dale said with a slight chuckle, though still defensive. "Statement pieces."

"They're a little ridiculous."

Dale looked at her, then back at his creations, then at her again. "A little?"

"Okay, a lot ridiculous." Donna picked up the Funnel Cake Spectacular. "But also... kind of impressive? I mean, how did you even get it to stand up like this?"

"Three wooden skewers and wishful thinking," Dale admitted. "Also, I may have used way too much caramel as structural support."

Donna examined it closer. "Dale, this thing weighs like five pounds."

"Seven, actually. I weighed it." He said it with such pride that Donna had to bite back another laugh.

"Who's going to eat a seven-pound funnel cake?"

"A very hungry person?" Dale offered. Then, more seriously but with a glint in his eye, "Okay, fine. Maybe I got a little carried away. But you have to admit, the flavors are solid."

"You know what Frank said to me when I fired him? He said I was stuck in the past. That I was too rigid, too afraid to evolve." Dale motioned around them. "So I evolved. Into this."

Donna raised an eyebrow. "You evolved into a mad scientist who builds funnel cake sculptures at four in the morning?"

"When you say it like that, it sounds less impressive."

"Dale." She set down the Funnel Cake Spectacular carefully. "You're a brilliant chef. But you're trying to beat him at his own game, and that's not a competition you can win, because it's his game, not yours."

Dale made a face. "The worst part? Everything he's doing actually works. I like to think I taught him something." He nodded toward the window with grudging respect. "The presentation, creating an experience—he's taken it all and made it his own. And he's doing it three stores down from us."

"So you're proud and annoyed at the same time?"

"Extremely." Dale picked at some powdered sugar on the counter. "Watching him push boundaries, try new things—it made me realize we've been playing it safe for years. Making the same funnel cakes, the same way, season after season." He waved at the mess. "So I went a little overboard trying to prove we could innovate too."

"Dale. Stop." Donna tried not to laugh as she looked at the swan creation. She picked it up carefully. The moment she lifted it, the whole thing collapsed in her hands, fried dough breaking apart and Madagascar vanilla pastry cream oozing everywhere. "See? Even your funnel cake swan is trying to tell you something."

Dale stared at the mess in her hands. "That was structurally sound five minutes ago."

"It was held together by hope and caramel."

"Those are legitimate binding agents in pastry," Dale protested, but he was fighting a smile now.

Donna set the swan remains on the counter. "Look, I get it. We both want to win. But turning our funnel cakes into avant-garde art installations isn't the answer."

"Then what is?" Dale leaned against the counter, looking at his creations. "Because right now, Frank's winning. Our sales are down thirty percent this week, Donna. Thirty percent."

"So we figure out how to win our way, not his way. This?

This is you trying to play his game. And yeah, I'm sure these taste amazing—"

"Thank you—"

"—but nobody's going to order this with a sparkler on top. At least not more than once."

Donna grabbed a fork and tried the Spectacular. "Oh wow, this honey lavender ice cream is insane. See? This is what you should be focusing on: making our funnel cakes the best tasting ones on the boardwalk, not the flashiest."

"Frank's are flashy and taste good," Dale pointed out.

"Frank's trying to do it all. We could be the best at one thing."

Dale considered this then looked around at the destroyed kitchen. "So you're saying I wasted six hours making edible architecture?"

"I'm saying you created some very delicious disasters." Donna took another bite of the Spectacular. "Wait, is there cardamom in this caramel?"

"Just a hint. You noticed?" Dale asked, clearly pleased.

"It's perfect." She pointed her fork at him. "That's what I'm talking about. This level of flavor—not seven-pound tower cakes."

Dale looked around at the disaster zone then back at Donna. "You want me to go home and sleep?"

"Yes." Donna set down her fork. "You're going to go home, take a shower, and get some actual sleep. And then we need to think of a way to revamp our funnel cake business without trying to be something we're not."

* * *

The sound of laughter drifted from the kitchen—Greg's voice mixing with Charlie's and Patrick's as they prepped for the lunch service. Both had worked under Greg at Heirloom and hadn't hesitated when he'd asked them to stay on for Furnish &

Feast. Liz paused in front of a shelf, adjusting the angle of a vintage brass candlestick, and smiled at the easy camaraderie filtering through the space. The rhythmic thunk of a knife against a cutting board punctuated their conversation, along with the occasional rush of water from the sink, all layered over the mellow sound of Fleetwood Mac playing softly from the café's speakers.

She stepped back to survey the display she'd been working on—a collection of ceramic planters in varying sizes and glazes, each one unique. The surfaces ranged from matte white to speckled blue-gray to a soft sage green with crackling. Next to them, she arranged a cluster of nautical rope-wrapped candlesticks and a few carefully chosen pieces of coastal drift-wood she collected from the beach last week.

It was still early, before the lunch crowd, giving her time to make these small adjustments that most customers would never consciously notice but that contributed to the overall feeling of the space. It was mid-May, and Cape May was just beginning to wake up for the season, with locals still outnumbering tourists, but the energy shifting as summer approached.

Speaking of which, the kitchen sounds had shifted from prep work banter to the more focused rhythm of actual cooking. She could hear Greg giving instructions, the hiss of something hitting a hot pan.

"Coffee's ready," Greg called out from the kitchen.

"Thanks," Liz called back.

A moment later, he emerged with two mugs, handing her one before taking a sip of his own. His hair was still damp from his shower, and he wore one of his chef's aprons. The apron was deep navy blue, a Christmas gift from Liz, embroidered with "Furnish & Feast" in cream thread.

"Charlie and Patrick are crushing it back there," he said, nodding toward the kitchen. "Got everything prepped and ready to go."

Liz took a sip of coffee. Perfect, as always. Greg still had his touch for the details that mattered.

"I'm going to prep the new salad," he said. "Jason said he wanted footage of the behind-the-scenes stuff, right? Might as well give him something worth filming."

Liz nodded and watched him disappear back into the kitchen. She turned her attention to her own workspace, the corner near the front where she'd set up her furniture restoration station. Today's project was a nightstand she'd found at an estate sale last weekend. It had good bones—solid wood construction, dovetail joints that spoke to quality craftsmanship. But someone had painted it an unfortunate shade of peach sometime in the eighties.

She'd already started the stripping process yesterday, and now the piece sat waiting, half the old paint removed and the other half still clinging stubbornly to the wood. Where she'd worked, the warm oak showed through, but plenty of paint remained around the edges and decorative details. Today she'd finish removing the rest, sand it smooth, and apply the first coat of stain.

At precisely two o'clock, Jason Potter arrived.

He came through the door with an energy that filled the room, not frantic or overwhelming, but purposeful and focused. His equipment spoke to serious intent: a DSLR camera hung from his neck, and he carried a canvas bag over one shoulder along with a collapsed ring light under his other arm.

Greg emerged from the kitchen, and they both greeted Jason.

"Liz, Greg," he said warmly, shaking their hands. "Thanks for doing this. I've been looking forward to it all week."

"We're happy to have you," Greg said confidently.

Jason spent the first few minutes just observing, walking through the space the way he had on opening day, but this time with a more analytical eye. He took test shots, checked the lighting from different angles, made notes on his phone.

"The natural light in here is fantastic," he said, looking up at the tall windows. "And I love how you've got the two sides working together—the café and the furniture shop. It's like they're in conversation with each other."

He turned to them with a smile. "Okay, here's how I usually work. I'm going to get some footage of you both doing what you do—Greg in the kitchen, Liz working on furniture. Then I'll do some sit-down interviews, get the story behind the place. And if any customers come in, I might ask if I can get their reaction to the space. Sound good?"

"Sounds perfect," Liz said.

"Great. Let's start in the kitchen."

Jason followed Greg behind the marble-topped counter, and Liz watched as her husband transformed into what she privately thought of as "Chef Greg," the version of himself that was most at home with a knife in his hand and ingredients spread before him.

"I'm prepping for lunch service," Greg explained to the camera, his voice relaxed and natural. "Everything here is made fresh daily. No shortcuts."

He'd set out his mise en place on the stainless steel counter: tomatoes still beaded with water from washing, a head of iceberg lettuce, several red bell peppers, fresh basil with leaves so green they looked almost artificial, a container of mayonnaise, and small bowls of spices.

Greg selected a bunch of radishes, their tops still vibrant and fresh, and placed them on the cutting board.

"These are from a farm about twenty minutes from here." He held up the bunch. "Look at the color—that deep pink-red. And the greens are still crisp, which means they were pulled this morning."

The knife moved with practiced precision. Greg trimmed the greens first, setting them aside in a small bowl. "These don't go to waste," he explained. "We'll use them in a pesto later this week." Then he began slicing the radishes themselves into thin, perfect rounds that revealed the white flesh beneath the colorful skin, each slice uniform and delicate.

He moved through the rest of the prep with the same care: butter lettuce separated leaf by tender leaf, sugar snap peas blanched for thirty seconds until they emerged bright green from an ice bath, a lemon vinaigrette whisked together until it emulsified into a pale yellow sauce.

"Spring vegetables are delicate," Greg explained. "You don't want to overpower them with a heavy dressing. This is bright, clean. It lets the vegetables shine."

He moved on to prep work for the sandwiches, and Jason captured it all: the practiced teamwork between Greg, Charlie, and Patrick, the careful plating, the attention to detail that made a simple lunch feel special.

A customer came in, a woman in her sixties with silver hair who introduced herself as Diana. Jason filmed her ordering. He captured Greg's relaxed manner as he made her cappuccino and plated her sandwich.

"It's not just food," Diana said when Jason asked about the café. "It's the whole experience. The care they take with everything. And look at this place! It's like having lunch in someone's beautiful home."

After he'd gotten enough footage of the café, Jason moved to Liz's corner.

"Okay," he said, "show me what you do."

Liz took a breath and turned to the nightstand. She laid out her tools the way she always did when working on a piece: paint stripper, putty knife, various grits of sandpaper, clean rags, the can of stain she'd selected, the small jar of new hardware still in its packaging.

"This is a nightstand I picked up at an estate sale last weekend," she began, running her hand along the top surface. "Solid oak construction, probably 1940s based on the joinery.

Someone had painted it peach." She pointed to the piece, where about half the paint had been stripped away. "I started yesterday, but there's still quite a bit left, especially around the edges and these decorative details where the paint really settled in."

She picked up the putty knife and began working on a stubborn section of paint near one of the drawer pulls. The old paint came away in curls and flakes, revealing the honey-colored oak beneath.

"The stripping process is actually my favorite part," she said, aware of the camera but trying to ignore it, focusing instead on the familiar rhythm of the work. "It's like archaeology. You're uncovering what was always there, what someone covered up."

She worked methodically, stripping, then sanding with progressively finer grits, answering Jason's questions about where she sourced pieces and what came next in the process.

When she'd finished the sanding and wiped the piece clean with a tack cloth, she opened the can of stain. The rich, woody smell filled her corner of the shop.

"This is the moment of truth," she said, dipping a clean rag into the stain. "This is where you see the transformation really start to happen."

She applied the stain in long, even strokes, working with the grain. The effect was immediate and dramatic. Where the raw sanded oak had been pale and uniform, the stain brought out rich variations in color: deeper browns in the grain lines, golden highlights where the wood was less dense. The wood seemed to come alive under her hands, showing patterns and character that had been hidden under layers of peach paint.

"It's incredible," he said softly. "You're literally bringing it back to life."

"That's the idea," Liz said, and found herself smiling.

Jason spent the next hour filming Liz as she went about her regular tasks, restocking displays, arranging vignettes, adjusting the placement of furniture and décor with the careful eye that made the space feel both curated and lived-in.

Then they moved outside for exterior shots. He filmed the soft-slate-blue facade, the cream shutters, the window boxes overflowing with pink geraniums. The front porch with its bistro tables and string lights overhead. The hand-lettered "Furnish & Feast" sign that managed to feel both classic and contemporary.

"This is perfect," he said finally. "The whole thing—inside and out. You've really brought your vision to life."

Back inside, Jason set up for the sit-down interviews while Charlie and Patrick handled the café. The conversation flowed naturally as Liz and Greg told the story of Furnish & Feast: the water damage setback, the decision to combine their passions, the joy of creating something sustainable and manageable after Greg's restaurant burnout.

"What do you hope people take away from this place?" Jason asked.

Liz and Greg exchanged a glance, one of those wordless communications that came from years together.

"I hope they see that beautiful things don't have to be brand new or wasteful," Liz said. "That there's value in restoration, in giving old things new purpose. That you can surround yourself with beauty in a sustainable way."

"And I hope they taste the difference that care makes," Greg added. "That they leave feeling nourished, not just fed. That they remember what it's like when food is made with attention and good ingredients, without all the fuss and pretension."

He smiled behind his camera. "That's beautiful. And I think that's exactly what's going to resonate with people."

By the time he packed up his equipment, it was nearly five o'clock. The afternoon had flown by in a blur of filming and conversation. Jason had a way of making them comfortable, of drawing out the authentic version of themselves rather than some performed, camera-ready persona.

"When will the video be up?" Greg asked as they walked Jason to the door.

"I'll need a few days to edit," Jason said. "Probably early next week. I'll send you the link as soon as it's live."

They shook hands, and Liz and Greg watched him walk down the street toward where he'd parked, unsure of what would happen next with the video.

CHAPTER SEVEN

The bus that picked up Chris and Sarah for the swamp tour was painted to look like an alligator. A massive, grinning alligator with teeth that wrapped around the front bumper and eyes that stared out from the hood. The words "Gator Gus's Bayou Adventures" were painted along the side in letters that looked like they were dripping with swamp water.

"This is amazing," Chris said, pulling out his phone to take a picture.

The bus driver, a woman who might have been sixty or might have been a hundred, leaned out the door. "You two Sarah and Chris?"

"That's us," Sarah said.

"Well, get on up here! We got a full load today, and Captain Gus don't wait for nobody!"

They climbed aboard to find every seat taken except for two near the back. The bus smelled like sunscreen and the kind of industrial air freshener that didn't quite cover up the underlying scent of mildew. Sarah made her way down the aisle, grabbing seat backs for balance as the driver pulled away from the curb before they'd even sat down.

And there, in the very back row, were Amber and Kevin.

"Oh my gosh!" Amber shrieked, loud enough that several passengers turned around. "You guys! What are the odds?"

Sarah felt Chris's hand on her lower back, a gentle pressure that said *we can survive this*. They made their way to the empty seats directly in front of Amber and Kevin.

"We didn't know you were doing the swamp tour today!" Amber was saying, leaning forward so her head was practically between them. "This is so crazy! Kevin, isn't this crazy?"

"Pretty crazy," Kevin agreed. He was wearing a hat that said "Gator Hunter" even though Sarah was fairly certain Kevin had never hunted anything in his life.

The bus lurched around a corner, and Amber let out a small yelp, steadying herself. "This is going to be amazing. The reviews said Captain Gus is hilarious and we might see baby alligators and there's this part where we go through the cypress swamp that's supposed to be super cool!"

The bus headed east out of the city, the buildings gradually giving way to industrial areas and then to stretches of wetland. Spanish moss hung from the trees, and every few minutes they'd pass a shack or a trailer sitting up on stilts, American flags and fishing nets decorating the porches.

Amber kept up a running commentary the entire way, pointing out things she'd read about in her research, asking the other passengers where they were from, and at one point standing up to take a panoramic video that required her to rotate slowly in place while everyone else tried not to get hit by her phone.

The bus finally pulled into a gravel parking lot next to a dock where a flat-bottomed airboat waited. The boat was covered with a green canopy to block the sun, and bench seats ran along both sides. At the back, on an elevated platform, sat what looked like an airplane propeller in a cage.

A man who could only be Captain Gus stood on the dock. He was exactly what Sarah had pictured: probably in his seventies, wearing overalls with no shirt underneath, deeply tanned skin that looked like leather, and a baseball cap with a stuffed baby alligator attached to the front.

"Alright, alright!" he called out as everyone filed off the bus. "Welcome to Gator Gus's Bayou Adventures! I'm Captain Gus, in case you couldn't figure that out from the sign. Now, who here's afraid of alligators?"

About half the group raised their hands, including Amber, who raised both hands.

"Good!" Captain Gus said. "You should be! Alligators'll eat anything. Dogs, cats, tourists from Ohio." He pointed at a family near the front. "You folks from Ohio?"

"Michigan," the father corrected.

"Close enough! They'll eat you too!" Captain Gus let out a laugh that sounded like a bullfrog. "Alright, everyone on the boat. Life jackets are required, and if you fall in, try to look like you taste bad."

They boarded the boat, which rocked alarmingly with each person who stepped aboard. Sarah grabbed the bench to steady herself. Chris sat next to her, and before she could stop it from happening, Amber and Kevin had claimed the spots right across from them.

"This is so exciting!" Amber said, struggling with her life jacket. "Kevin, can you help me with this buckle? I can't get it to— there we go! Sarah, are you excited?"

"Very excited," Sarah said, and she was, despite everything. This was ridiculous and touristy and perfect.

Captain Gus climbed up to his platform, and without warning, the propeller roared to life. The sound was deafening, like standing behind a jet engine. Sarah felt the vibration in her chest. Captain Gus gave them a thumbs-up and a grin that showed several missing teeth, then they were moving.

The boat shot forward, skimming across the water so fast that Sarah's stomach dropped. They careened around a bend, Spanish moss whipping past close enough to touch. The wind created by the propeller and their speed made it impossible to hear anything except the roar of the engine.

Amber was screaming. Not in fear—in pure, unbridled joy. Her phone was out, recording everything, her hair whipping around her face.

They slowed as they entered a narrower channel, the cypress trees closing in on both sides. The propeller quieted to a manageable rumble, and Captain Gus's voice came over a crackling speaker system.

The heat settled over them immediately now that they weren't moving. It was humid and thick, the kind of swamp air that made Sarah's shirt stick to her back. Even under the canopy, the sun felt relentless.

"Now see them trees there? Them's bald cypress, been here longer than anybody's great-great-granddaddy. And you see them knees?" He pointed to the knobby protrusions sticking up from the water. "Them's called cypress knees, and they help the tree breathe. Kind of like a snorkel."

He steered them deeper into the swamp. The water was dark, almost black, and perfectly still except for their wake. Lily pads floated on the surface, and every now and then Sarah would see something move beneath the water.

"Now keep your eyes peeled," Captain Gus said. "Gators like to sun themselves on logs this time of day. If you see one, don't stick your hand in the water. Unless you only need nine fingers."

Everyone laughed nervously and pulled their hands closer to their bodies.

They drifted around another bend, the propeller barely turning, and there it was. An alligator, massive and still, lying on a partially submerged log. Its eyes were closed, its body perfectly still except for the slow rise and fall of its breathing.

"Oh my gosh oh my gosh oh my gosh," Amber whispered, which for her was practically silent. She had her phone up, zoomed in as far as it would go.

Captain Gus cut the engine completely, and they floated closer. The alligator didn't move.

"That there's Beauregard," Captain Gus said softly. "He's been living in this stretch of swamp for about thirty years. Named him myself. He's about twelve feet long, which for a gator is pretty respectable. Now watch this."

He pulled a bag of marshmallows from under his seat. "This is how we get him to wake up and say hello."

He tossed a marshmallow toward the log. It landed in the water with a soft plop about ten feet from the alligator.

For a moment, nothing happened. Then Beauregard's eyes opened. He moved so fast Sarah didn't even see it happen— one second he was on the log, the next he was in the water, jaws snapping closed on the marshmallow. The sound of his jaws closing was like a car door slamming.

Everyone on the boat gasped. Amber actually screamed.

Beauregard surfaced, shook his head once, and then slid back under the water, disappearing completely.

"And that," Captain Gus said cheerfully, "is why we don't swim in the bayou."

They continued on, seeing more alligators—some small, some massive, one that Captain Gus claimed was over fifteen feet long though Sarah couldn't see all of it. They saw snowy egrets perched in the trees, a great blue heron that took flight as they approached, and something Captain Gus identified as a cottonmouth snake sunning itself on a branch.

"Them's venomous," he said casually. "Real venomous. Best to leave 'em alone."

They headed back toward the dock, the propeller roaring to life again, the boat skimming across the water. This time Sarah was ready for the speed, and she found herself laughing as the boat bounced over the choppy water, spray flying up on both sides.

Back on solid ground, everyone climbed off the boat, legs shaky from the ride. Sarah's shirt was damp with sweat and spray, and she could already feel the sunburn starting on her nose despite the canopy on the boat.

On the bus ride back to the city, Amber couldn't stop talking about everything they'd seen.

"That was AMAZING!" she said loudly enough that several passengers turned around. "Kevin, wasn't that amazing? Did you see how close that alligator got? I thought it was going to eat the marshmallow right out of Captain Gus's hand! And that snake—what was it called? A cottonmouth? I've never seen a real venomous snake before!"

The bus pulled back into the French Quarter, dropping them off at the same corner where it had picked them up that morning. As everyone got off, Sarah and Chris found themselves walking back to Maison Beaumont alongside Amber and Kevin.

They reached the guest house, and Amber and Kevin headed toward their room while Sarah and Chris went to theirs.

"See you guys later!" Amber called over her shoulder.

Once inside their room with the door closed, Chris let out a long breath. "Nice people."

"Very nice," Sarah agreed. "Just... a lot."

"Exactly."

They showered and changed, getting ready to venture out to Bourbon Street on their own.

Bourbon Street at night was exactly what Sarah had expected and somehow still more. The smell hit them first—beer, sweat, fried food, and something sweet she couldn't identify. Music poured out of every doorway, competing for dominance. A jazz band here, rock cover band there, someone's terrible karaoke attempt from a third-floor balcony.

People were everywhere. Tourists stumbling with enormous

frozen drinks in hand, bachelorette parties in matching T-shirts, street performers juggling fire, a man dressed as a statue who kept perfectly still until someone dropped money in his bucket.

"This is insane," Chris said, pulling Sarah closer as they navigated through the crowd.

They ducked into a bar called The Cat's Meow, where people were dancing on tables to "Sweet Caroline." A woman in a feather boa grabbed Sarah's hand and tried to pull her up to join them. Sarah laughed and shook her head, pointing to Chris as an excuse.

Back on the street, they passed a fortune teller with tarot cards spread on a velvet cloth, a hot dog vendor, three different souvenir shops all selling the same Mardi Gras beads and voodoo dolls. Someone handed Chris a flyer for a strip club. Someone else tried to sell them something called a "Hand Grenade" in a massive plastic cup.

"Should we get drinks?" Sarah asked.

"Definitely."

They ended up at a place called Lafitte's Blacksmith Shop Bar, supposedly one of the oldest bars in America. It was dark inside, lit only by candles, and significantly quieter than the chaos outside. They ordered Hurricanes and found a spot near the back.

"This is better," Sarah said, taking a sip. The drink was sweet and strong, tasting like fruit punch with a serious kick.

"Much better," Chris agreed. "Though I feel like we're missing out on the authentic Bourbon Street experience by not being completely wasted and wearing plastic beads."

They stayed for two drinks then ventured back out into the madness. The crowd had grown even larger, and Sarah found herself pressed against Chris as they moved down the street. A group dressed as superheroes pushed past them. Someone was selling roses.

They stopped to watch a brass band playing on the corner,

the music so loud Sarah could feel it in her chest. People were dancing, and before she knew it, Chris had pulled her into the crowd and they were dancing too, laughing as they tried to keep rhythm with the music.

When the song ended, they kept walking, turning down a side street that was slightly less crowded. They found a restaurant called Acme Oyster House with a line out the door.

"Worth it?" Chris asked.

"Definitely."

They waited in line for twenty minutes then scored seats at the bar. Sarah ordered chargrilled oysters, and Chris got a po'boy, and they both agreed it was some of the best food they'd eaten all trip.

It was past midnight when they finally headed back toward Maison Beaumont, both exhausted. Sarah's feet hurt from walking, and she was pretty sure she had a blister forming on her heel.

Back in their room, Sarah sank into the chair by the window and bent down to unlace her shoes with relief. Chris went to the bathroom. She pulled off one shoe then the other, wiggling her sore toes.

She twisted her wedding band absently, the way she'd been doing since they got married. Still getting used to the weight of it. Still getting used to being married.

Except when she looked down, her engagement ring was gone.

Sarah sat up, her heart suddenly pounding. She looked at her hand again, hoping she was mistaken. But no—the wedding band was there, but the engagement ring that was supposed to sit above it was missing.

"Chris."

He came out of the bathroom. "Yeah?"

"My ring is gone."

"What?"

She held up her hand. "My engagement ring. It's gone."

Chris crossed the room in two steps, taking her hand and examining it as if the ring might somehow be hiding. "When did you last see it?"

"I don't know. I wasn't paying attention. It was there this morning, I know it was."

Sarah tried to remember. Had she noticed it at dinner? On Bourbon Street? During the swamp tour? She'd been twisting both rings together, she was sure of it. But when?

"Maybe it's here somewhere," Chris said, already scanning the floor. "Maybe it fell off when you took off your shoes."

They searched the room. Under the bed, in the bathroom, in their bags, in the pockets of the clothes they'd worn earlier. Nothing.

"The hot tub," Sarah said suddenly. "Last night. What if it came off in the hot tub?"

They went out to the courtyard, but the hot tub was dark now, the water still. Chris turned on the light and they both peered into it, but the ring wasn't visible on the bottom.

"It has to be on Bourbon Street," Sarah said, feeling sick. "It must have slipped off when we were walking or dancing or—"

"Okay," Chris said calmly, though Sarah could see the worry in his eyes. "Okay. We'll retrace our steps. We'll find it."

"Chris, it's after midnight. Bourbon Street is packed. Even if we go back, how are we supposed to find a tiny ring in all that chaos?"

"We start with the places we stopped. The bars, the restaurant. Someone might have turned it in."

Sarah wanted to cry. The ring he'd saved for months to buy. The ring she'd been wearing for less than a year.

"We'll find it," Chris said again. "Come on. Let's go look around outside. Maybe it fell off when we were walking back."

They grabbed a flashlight from their room and headed out to the courtyard. Sarah's eyes scanned the brick pathways, the area around the hot tub, anywhere the ring might have fallen.

"Check the driveway," Chris suggested. "We walked through there when we came back."

Sarah walked to the front of the guest house, shining the flashlight on the gravel driveway. And there, catching the light, was a glint of something metallic.

Her ring.

She picked it up, relief flooding through her. "Chris! I found it!"

He came around the corner. "Seriously?"

"It was right here." She slipped the ring back on her finger, checking to make sure it was secure. "I must have been fidgeting with it when we got back and it fell off."

"Thank god," Chris said. "I was not looking forward to retracing our steps through all of Bourbon Street."

They returned inside, Sarah keeping her hand in a fist just to be safe. Back in their room, she felt the exhaustion hit her all at once.

Chris opened the French doors to let in some air, and Sarah changed into pajamas. She was just brushing her teeth when she heard it.

Footsteps.

Not from the courtyard or the street. From inside their room. Slow, deliberate footsteps crossing the hardwood floor.

Sarah came out of the bathroom, toothbrush still in hand. "Chris?"

He was standing in the middle of the room, looking around. "You heard that too?"

"Yeah."

The footsteps stopped near the doors. They stared at the open doorway, at the gauzy curtains moving slightly in the breeze.

And then the doors slammed shut.

Both of them jumped. The sound echoed through the room, loud and violent, nothing like the gentle swing of a door caught by the wind.

"That was... that was something," Chris said, his voice shaky.

Before Sarah could respond, the bathroom door swung open. Then slowly closed again.

The lamp on the nightstand flickered. Once. Twice. Then went out completely.

"Outside. Now," Chris said.

They didn't need to discuss it. Both of them hurried through the doors into the courtyard. The night air was warm and still. Sarah took a deep breath, her heart still pounding.

"That was real, right?" she said. "You saw that too?"

"I saw it."

They stood there for a moment, neither of them wanting to go back inside.

"Sarah? Chris?"

They turned. Amber and Kevin were standing in their doorway across the courtyard, wrapped in robes.

Amber and Kevin crossed the courtyard to join them. Kevin looked pale, and Amber's usual enthusiasm was notably absent.

"This place is haunted," Amber said flatly. "Our room is definitely haunted."

"What's been happening in your room?" Chris asked.

"Doors opening and closing," Kevin said. "Things moving. We heard someone walking around earlier, but when we looked, no one was there."

"The lights keep flickering," Amber added. "And Kevin's phone died even though it was fully charged, and when he plugged it in, it wouldn't charge. Then five minutes later it was working fine."

They all stood there, looking at each other in the dim light from the courtyard lamps.

"Maybe we should all just sit out here for a while," Sarah suggested. "Safety in numbers?"

"Good idea," Kevin said. "I'm definitely not going back in our room alone right now."

"The hot tub?" Amber suggested, pointing to it in the corner of the courtyard.

They all walked over. Chris checked the temperature. "It's on. Still warm from earlier."

"I could use a drink anyway," Kevin said.

They went to their respective rooms to quickly change into swimsuits and grab drinks, none of them wanting to linger inside. Sarah hurried to find the champagne they'd opened last night and brought it out along with plastic cups from the bathroom.

When they were all settled in the hot tub, Amber took a long sip of her drink and said, "So we're all in agreement that this place is haunted, right? Like, seriously haunted?"

"The cab driver told us a jazz musician died here in the thirties," Sarah said. "Said he still plays trumpet."

"We've been hearing trumpet," Chris confirmed. "Last night and tonight."

"We heard it too," Kevin said. "Thought it was coming from outside, but..."

"But it's not," Amber finished.

They sat in silence for a moment, the only sound the bubbles from the hot tub jets.

"Look," Kevin said suddenly, pointing toward Sarah and Chris's room.

They all turned. Through the open French doors, they could see into their room. The lamp they'd left off was on now. As they watched, it flickered. Then the bathroom light turned on. Then off. Then on again.

"Okay, that's not normal," Amber said.

The lights continued their pattern—on, off, on, off—like someone was playing with the switches. Then, slowly, the doors began to swing closed. Not like they were being pushed by wind. Deliberately. Smoothly.

They closed completely.

They all stared at the closed doors, waiting to see if anything else would happen. The room was still now, silent.

"I think," Amber said slowly, "we should maybe tell the front desk in the morning."

"Yeah," Sarah agreed, her voice shaky. "That sounds like a good idea."

They stayed in the hot tub for another hour, none of them wanting to be the first to go back inside. They talked in quiet voices about what they'd seen, trying to rationalize it, failing to do so.

Finally, exhaustion won. They said goodnight and retreated to their rooms, Sarah and Chris leaving their French doors open despite everything, both of them feeling like they needed an escape route.

Sarah lay in bed next to Chris, both of them staring at the ceiling.

"Did that really just happen?" she asked.

"I think so."

"We're going to look back on this honeymoon and laugh, right?"

"Eventually," Chris said. "Maybe in about twenty years."

Sarah closed her eyes. She'd lost her engagement ring. They'd witnessed an actual haunting.

This was definitely going to be a honeymoon they'd never forget.

CHAPTER EIGHT

Lisa drove to the oyster farm that morning. She'd spent the last five days staring at the preliminary information from Tidal Wave Sports, the acquisition offer burning a hole through her laptop screen.

Nick was at the dock, boots crusted with mud, clipboard in hand. Aaron and another worker were out checking the beds.

"Hey," he said. His face was drawn, worry lines deeper than before.

"How are the oysters?"

"Not great. The biologist just left—she took more samples, thinks it might be bacterial. Lab results should be back in a few days." He rubbed his jaw. "But we found something else this morning. Come look."

He led her down the dock to where one of the mesh marker buoys should have been. Instead, there was just an empty section of water.

"Someone cut the buoy line," Nick said. "And look over there." He pointed to another spot about twenty feet away. "That line's been moved. Someone's been messing with my markers. If I lose track of where my lease boundaries are, boats could damage the beds, and I can't keep track of which areas I've already checked."

Lisa stared at the water. "Who would do this?"

"I don't know. The conservation officers took a report when we found the traps last time, but they haven't turned up anything." He grabbed a length of frayed rope from the dock. "I think this is deliberate, Lisa. Someone's trying to sabotage my operation."

Aaron called over from one of the beds. "Nick! You need to see this!"

They walked to the edge of the dock where Aaron was standing in his waders, holding up a mesh bag. Even from a distance, Lisa could see something was wrong.

"This bag's been cut open," Aaron said. "And there's at least thirty oysters missing. Someone's been poaching."

Nick stiffened. He took the bag from Aaron, examining the clean slice through the mesh. "How many bags did you check?"

"Just started this section. But if they hit here, they probably hit the other beds too."

"Check them all," Nick said quietly. "Document everything."

Aaron gave a quick nod and waded back out into the water. Nick stood there, turning the damaged bag over in his hands.

Lisa didn't know what to say.

He dropped the bag back into the water and looked at her. "Between the dying oysters and this? I'm starting to think someone really doesn't want me here."

Inside the office shed, Nick poured them both coffee from a dented thermos.

"There's something I need to tell you," Lisa said.

Nick looked up. "OK."

She took a breath. "I got a call five days ago. From Tidal Wave Sports. They want to buy my business, Current Culture." She paused. "I didn't tell you because I needed time to think about it on my own first. Without anyone else's input."

Nick's eyes widened. "Lisa, that's incredible. What did they say?"

She explained everything. The offer, the two options, what the preliminary information showed, the invitation to fly out to San Diego to discuss it all in person. When she finished, Nick was staring at her with surprise and pride.

"Lisa, that could be a major opportunity."

"I know," Lisa said.

"So why do you look unsure?" Nick asked.

She set down her coffee. "Because what if they compromise everything I've built? I care about actually protecting the ocean, not just slapping 'eco-friendly' on a label. What if they pressure me to cut corners on sustainability to boost profits?"

"That's fair," Nick said. "So make that clear in San Diego. Tell them your standards aren't negotiable. If they want Current Culture, they get the real thing, not some compromised version."

"True," she said. "But what if they say yes now and change things later?"

"Build that into the contract. You're putting everything back into the business, aren't you? Living lean while Current Culture grows?"

She nodded. "Every dollar."

"So you have leverage. They want what you've built. Make them protect it."

Her phone buzzed in her pocket. She pulled it out and saw Rebecca Nixon's name on the screen.

"It's them," she said.

"Answer it."

Lisa took a breath and swiped to accept. "Hello?"

"Lisa! Hi, it's Rebecca. I hope I'm not catching you at a bad time?"

"No, it's fine."

"Great. I wanted to check in. We sent over the preliminary information earlier this week, and I know this is a big decision.

I'm hoping you've had a chance to think about flying out to meet the team?"

Lisa looked at Nick. He nodded, mouthed the words *do it*.

"Actually," Lisa said, "yes. I'd like to come out. When were you thinking?"

"How about tonight?" Rebecca's voice brightened. "I know it's last minute—I know we originally talked about next week, but our VP of Product Development just found out he has to leave for a trade show in Australia on Monday. If we can get you out here this weekend, the whole leadership team can meet with you. Otherwise we're looking at three weeks from now, and honestly, I don't want to wait that long. We have a flight leaving Philadelphia at 8:45 PM. Gets you into San Diego around midnight local time. We'd put you up at the Pendry, right downtown, and we could meet first thing tomorrow morning. What do you say?"

Lisa checked her watch. It was 9:30 AM. "Tonight?"

Nick raised his eyebrows, a small smile playing at his lips.

"OK," Lisa said. "Let's do it."

"Fantastic! I'm texting you the car service details right now. They'll pick you up at your place at 5:00 PM. That'll get you to Philadelphia with plenty of time. Pack for two nights, business casual. And Lisa? This is going to be great. I can't wait for you to see what we're building here."

"Thanks, Rebecca. I'll see you tomorrow."

Lisa hung up and stared at her phone. "I'm going to San Diego. Tonight."

Nick grinned and held up his hand for a high five. "You're going to kill it."

As she walked back to her car, she heard Nick's phone ring. He answered, and she paused, watching as he talked. His expression shifted—some of the tension leaving his face. When he hung up, he called over to her. "That was the researcher from Rutgers," he said. "The lab rushed the water quality results. She's got some preliminary findings and wants to talk through them tomorrow."

Lisa felt a weight lift slightly. At least Nick was getting somewhere. She got in her car and drove home to pack for a meeting that might decide the future of everything she'd built.

* * *

Judy and Bob were back at the lighthouse, binoculars hanging around both their necks. The climb was harder this time. Their muscles protested with each step, but they pushed through, driven by a need to see if anything else would happen at the bunker.

When they finally stepped out onto the watch gallery, Bob didn't pause to admire the view. He moved directly to the railing on the ocean side and raised the binoculars.

The bunker came into sharp focus through the lenses. He could see the weathered concrete walls, the rusting metal reinforcements, the dark gap on the seaward side where the figure had entered. Bob scanned the beach around it slowly, methodically. No one was there now. The sand looked undisturbed in the morning light.

He shifted his view north, searching for the spot where the person had been digging. There. About thirty yards from the bunker, near the taller beach grass. The driftwood was still there, arranged in that same deliberate pattern.

"See anything?" Judy asked quietly, raising her own binoculars to scan the beach.

"The marker's still there. But no one is around." Bob lowered the binoculars for a moment then raised them again to scan the water.

Several boats dotted the horizon—fishing vessels mostly, recreational boats farther out. Nothing unusual at first glance. He swept slowly across the ocean from south to north, adjusting the focus as he went.

That was when he saw it.

A small boat, white with blue trim, sitting perhaps a quarter mile offshore. It wasn't moving. Bob adjusted the focus, bringing the vessel into sharper detail. A single person stood at the bow, facing the shore, holding binoculars.

As Bob fine-tuned the focus, he could make out more details. There were numbers on the hull—a registration. He squinted, trying to read them. "NJ... 4827... ZY," he muttered under his breath, committing them to memory.

Bob was about to lower his own binoculars when movement near the bunker caught his eye. He swung his view back to the beach.

Two figures in dark clothing had appeared near the driftwood marker in the dunes. Bob's pulse quickened. One person crouched down and started digging while the other stood watch, scanning the beach in both directions.

"Judy," Bob said quietly.

"What?"

"Two people. At the burial spot."

Bob watched them through the lenses. The person digging worked quickly, their hands moving through the sand. The second person remained standing, checking their watch, then looking out at the water. The lookout raised a hand—some kind of signal.

After about thirty seconds, the digger pulled something out —a dark bundle or package—and examined it briefly before tucking it into their backpack. But before they covered it completely, Bob caught a glimpse in the sunlight. It wasn't just a bundle. It was rectangular, hard-sided, like a small case or container. The kind of thing you'd use to protect something valuable or fragile.

"Did you see that?" Bob asked quietly.

Judy focused her lenses on the scene. "What was it?"

"Looked like a case. Metal or hard plastic, maybe."

The digger straightened up. One of them raised binoculars and turned to face the ocean.

For a long moment, the person on the beach and the person on the boat stood perfectly still, looking at each other across the water. Bob felt like he was watching a silent conversation, some kind of confirmation or signal passing between them.

The figure on the beach lowered their binoculars first, said something to their companion, then both of them started walking north along the dunes. But they didn't leave. About fifty yards from the bunker, they stopped at a spot deeper in the dunes, near a distinctive grouping of rocks.

Bob followed their movements. One person pulled a container from their backpack—a different one, Bob noticed, smaller than what they'd retrieved. They knelt down and began working the sand while the other kept watch.

"They're burying something else," Bob said quietly.

Judy peered through her lenses. "A different spot this time."

Within a minute, they'd buried the container and covered it with sand. One of them picked up a piece of driftwood and stuck it upright in the sand, then placed a smaller piece across it at an angle. A marker, just like before. They rose, brushed themselves off, and continued walking north along the beach until they disappeared from view.

Bob continued watching the beach. His hands were shaking slightly. Judy lowered her own binoculars, her expression tense.

"They dug something up," Judy said. "Probably the thing that was buried the other day."

"And the boat was watching the whole time." Bob turned his attention back to the water. The boat's engine had started—he could see the white churn of water at the stern. The vessel turned slowly, heading north along the coast, picking up speed as it went.

"The boat's leaving," Bob said.

Judy kept her binoculars on it, watching as the boat picked

up speed, becoming smaller against the horizon. Within a minute, it had vanished around the curve of the coastline.

They both lowered their binoculars. Bob surveyed the shoreline below with his naked eye now. A few people walked along the beach farther south, near the parking area—a couple holding hands, someone jogging. But none of them seemed interested in the bunker or the area north of it.

Bob glanced at his watch. 10:23 AM. He committed the details to memory—the boat registration NJ4827ZY, the time, the two people, that metal case they'd retrieved from the first spot in the dunes. And now a second burial spot, about fifty yards north of the bunker, deeper in the dunes near those distinctive rocks.

"What are you thinking?" Bob asked Judy.

She was looking at the bunker, her brow furrowed. "I'm thinking about why someone would hide something there, mark the spot, and have someone else watching from the water."

"It's definitely coordinated," Bob said. "Whatever it is."

Judy lowered her binoculars and turned to him. "You know what it reminds me of? That geocaching thing our grandkids are always doing. Hiding things, marking coordinates, finding them later."

Bob considered that. "Could be some kind of game or treasure hunt."

"With a boat as part of it?" Judy said. "That would be pretty elaborate."

"People do all kinds of things for hobbies," Bob said. He glanced back at the beach. "Though I'll admit, the whole thing does seem... I don't know. Official, almost. The way they moved, the timing."

"Maybe it's a competition or something," Judy offered. "One of those adventure race things."

They stood in silence for a moment, both trying to make sense of what they'd witnessed.

Behind them, voices rose as more visitors emerged onto the watch gallery. A group of teenagers spilled out, immediately pulling out their phones to take photos. An elderly man with a thick white beard positioned himself at the railing to Bob's left, spreading out a map.

Within minutes, the watch gallery had transformed from their private observation post to a crowded viewing platform. A woman with a toddler squeezed between Bob and Judy to point out a sailboat. Two middle-aged men in matching polo shirts debated whether they could see Delaware across the bay.

"This is getting crowded," Judy said, glancing at the growing number of people around them.

Bob agreed. Whatever they'd just witnessed felt deliberate and practiced. The coordination, the retrieval, the boat leaving. Not something amateurs would do.

Bob took one last look at the bunker below then followed Judy back toward the stairwell.

* * *

Margaret was in the kitchen, prepping vegetables for the barbecue they were hosting that afternoon, when she heard voices outside, loud and carefree, voices that didn't belong in their backyard. She moved to the window and watched as a group of six people, all in their twenties, had stopped right in the middle of the lawn. They'd set down their coolers and beach bags and were reorganizing their supplies, laughing and talking as if they were in a park. One of the guys shook sand out of a towel onto their grass. Another was digging through a cooler, tossing aside empty beer cans that landed on the lawn.

"Dave," she called.

He appeared from the dining room where he'd been setting up the folding tables they'd borrowed from Rob. "What's up?"

"Look."

They watched together as the group finally gathered their

things and moved toward the gate, leaving behind two crushed beer cans and a plastic bag that tumbled across the grass in the breeze.

Dave sighed, heading out to pick up the trash. "How many groups is that today?"

"Four, I think?" Margaret said. "And it's not even noon."

An hour later, Margaret was upstairs making the beds when she glanced out the window and saw another family cutting through. Mom, dad, and two elementary-aged kids with beach chairs and a wagon full of toys. They paused in the middle of the lawn to rearrange their supplies, the kids running in circles while the parents reorganized.

By the end of the day, they'd counted nine separate groups cutting through. Most just walked straight to the beach without incident, but several had stopped to reorganize their belongings, leaving behind various bits of trash.

"We should mention this at the barbecue," Margaret said as they continued prepping. She was slicing watermelon while Dave marinated chicken. "Maybe the neighbors will have some ideas."

Dave agreed. "Yeah, I'm curious if anyone else deals with this."

By two o'clock that afternoon, their backyard was full of neighbors. Dave manned the grill, flipping burgers and hot dogs while Billy stood beside him chatting. The kids, Harper, Abby, and Gloria's teenagers, were playing cornhole near the back fence. Valerie and Mary were setting out side dishes on the picnic table they'd borrowed from Rob, while Delores and Gloria relaxed in lawn chairs with sweating glasses of lemonade.

Margaret was bringing out a platter of sliced watermelon when she heard Mary's voice rise slightly.

"Oh, here we go."

Everyone turned to look. A group of college-aged kids were cutting through the yard. Maybe five or six of them, beach chairs and coolers in hand. They walked with the confidence of people who'd done this a hundred times before, barely glancing at the gathering of neighbors watching them.

"Excuse me," Dave called out from the grill, spatula still in hand.

The group slowed but didn't stop. One of the guys, tall and wearing board shorts and sunglasses, half-turned. "What's up?"

"This is private property," Dave said, keeping his voice even. "The public beach access is two blocks down."

"We're just going to the beach, dude," the guy said, already turning away. "We're not bothering anyone."

"You're cutting through my yard," Dave said, louder now.

"The beach belongs to everyone," one of the girls called back without even turning around. They kept walking, pushing through the gate and disappearing down the path.

For a moment, no one said anything. Then Billy let out a low whistle.

"That's exactly what I was talking about," Artie said, shaking his head. "That same attitude. Like because they paid to park somewhere, they own the whole town."

"How often is this happening?" Valerie asked, turning to Margaret.

"Constantly," Margaret said, setting down the watermelon. "The other day we counted nine groups. And some of them stop and set up right here on the lawn, leave trash, reorganize their coolers. It's like they think this is a public park."

"You need to lock that gate," Rob said immediately. He was a decisive man, always quick with solutions. "Get one of those keypad locks for the gate. Give the code to everyone on this block who uses the path legitimately, and keep everyone else out."

"I don't know," Margaret said slowly. "That feels extreme."

"It's not extreme," Gloria said. "It's practical. We all use that path to get to the beach. It's one of the perks that makes these houses worth what they are. But that doesn't mean random strangers get to traipse through your yard whenever they feel like it."

"The police won't do anything," Billy added. "I've called them before about this exact thing. They'll come out, tell people to move along, but they can't camp out here all day. A locked gate is the only real solution."

"Right now you have no control over who's coming through," Rob said. "At least with a lock, you decide."

Margaret looked at Dave, trying to read his expression. She could see him working through it, weighing the practicality versus the principle, the solution versus what it represented.

Dave nodded. "That makes sense," he said. "We'll get a lock. It's much cheaper than a new fence."

"Good call," Rob said, clapping him on the shoulder. "I'll text you the brand we used. Easy to install, weatherproof, the code system works great."

"And we'll add you both to the neighborhood group text," Gloria added. "That's how we share the code and coordinate path maintenance and everything. Right around now in May is when we start needing to use the lock with summer crowds."

Dave was quiet for a moment then let out a breath. "Can I ask you guys something else?"

"Of course," Mary said.

"For those of you who have other places - how do you balance being here versus being there?" He glanced at Margaret. "We have our house in West Cape May, and it's been tricky to manage. We've been spending so much time here on weekends that I feel like we're neglecting it. Like we're never really settled in either place."

Billy leaned back in his chair. "That's the second-home struggle. Delores and I dealt with that for years when we had our place upstate."

"What did you do?" Margaret asked.

"Eventually sold it," Delores said with a laugh. "But that

was after we retired. When we were still working, we had to be really intentional about schedules."

"We do every other weekend," Valerie offered. "Alternate between here and our place in Philly. It helps us not feel guilty about either place."

"That's smart," Dave said, sounding relieved. "We've just been coming here every weekend since we bought it, and I think that's part of the problem."

"You need a system," Rob said. "Mary and I used to do the same thing when we first bought here—came every single weekend, ran ourselves ragged. Now we're more intentional. Some weekends we stay home, take care of the yard, see our friends there. And we let friends and family use this place a weekend here or there—gives us a break and makes us feel less guilty about not being here."

"The house doesn't run away," Mary added. "It'll be here when you come back."

Margaret watched Dave's shoulders relax slightly. "Yeah, you're right. We just need a better schedule."

"First summer's always the hardest," Gloria said. "You want to be here all the time because it's new and exciting. But you'll find your rhythm."

Margaret felt relieved. They had solutions now—for the gate, for the schedule, for finding balance between both homes.

"Who wants a burger?" Dave called out, turning back to the grill. "They're ready."

The conversation shifted, the mood lightened, and soon everyone was eating and laughing again.

CHAPTER NINE

The email arrived at 6:47 AM.

Liz saw it first when she and Greg got to Furnish & Feast to start their day. She'd been checking her phone while Greg unlocked the front door, the morning still quiet on the street, just a few early joggers and the occasional car passing by.

Subject: Your video is LIVE! - Jason Potter

She opened it.

Hey Liz and Greg!

The video dropped yesterday morning and I honestly cannot believe what's happening. We're already past 500K views in less than 24 hours. My usual videos hit maybe 200-300K in the first week if I'm lucky. This is insane.

I think it's the authenticity. People are LOVING the combination of the café and the furniture restoration, the whole sustainable angle, the fact that you're doing something real in a world that feels increasingly disposable. Plus the space is just gorgeous on camera. I knew it would resonate, but this is next level.

Anyway, here's the link. Hope you're ready for some attention!

Best, Jason

Liz clicked the link, and her phone immediately opened YouTube. The thumbnail showed their storefront—slate-blue paint, cream shutters, pink geraniums spilling from the window boxes, the hand-lettered sign hanging above the door. It looked impossibly charming, like something from a magazine spread.

The title read: "This Café + Furniture Shop is Saving Cape May (And It's GORGEOUS)"
Views: 523,481

Her stomach did a small flip.

"What is it?" Greg asked, flipping on the lights.

"Come look at this." She held up her phone.

He came over to where she stood near the front counter. She handed him the phone.

She watched his face as he read Jason's email, saw his eyebrows climb as he registered the view count.

"Half a million," he said slowly. "In less than a day."

"It went live yesterday morning."

"Wow." He looked up from the phone. "Should we watch it?"

"I think we have to."

Greg started the coffee brewing in the kitchen while Liz grabbed his laptop from behind the counter. They settled at one of the small café tables, the morning light streaming through the tall windows. They pulled up the video, the laptop screen between them.

Jason's familiar face appeared first, speaking directly to the camera with the easy confidence of someone who'd done this hundreds of times.

"Hey everyone, Jason here. Today I'm in Cape May, New Jersey, and I just stumbled onto something really special. This place wasn't even on my list, but sometimes the best discoveries are the ones you don't plan for."

The video cut to exterior shots of Furnish & Feast—the facade they'd labored over, the porch with its bistro tables. Jason's voice continued over the footage.

"Meet Furnish & Feast, a business that's part café, part furniture restoration shop, and one hundred percent proof that good things can come from taking risks."

They watched as Jason's editing wove together everything he'd filmed. Liz working on the nightstand, the wood transforming under her hands. Greg's knife work in the kitchen, the vibrant spring vegetables. The interviews where their words came out sounding more thoughtful than they'd felt in the moment, Jason's editing giving weight to ideas they'd expressed almost casually.

"He made it look..." Liz started, then stopped, not quite sure how to finish.

"Professional," Greg said quietly. "Really professional."

The pacing was perfect, the background music warm and acoustic without overwhelming the content. Near the end, there was footage of them that Liz had forgotten about—Jason must have filmed it when they weren't paying attention. Greg was showing her something in the kitchen, both of them laughing, and the ease between them was palpable.

"What struck me most," Jason said in the video's conclusion, "was how Liz and Greg have created something that honors both craft and community. They're not trying to be everything to everyone. They're just doing what they love, doing it well, and creating a space where beauty and sustainability aren't luxuries—they're just how things are done."

The video ended with a final shot of the storefront in afternoon light, the sun making the blue paint look almost luminous.

Greg and Liz sat in silence for a long moment after the video ended.

"That was..." Liz started, then stopped. "I didn't realize it would be like that."

"He made us look good," Greg said quietly.

Liz scrolled down to the comments section, which was already overflowing.

This is exactly what small business should be. Quality over quantity, craft over consumption.

I live for content like this. The world needs more spaces like Furnish & Feast.

That furniture restoration was so satisfying to watch. I could watch an entire channel of just that.

The way they look at each other at 8:34... that's relationship goals right there.

I'm booking a trip to Cape May just to visit this place.

As someone who burned out of corporate America, Greg's story really resonates. You CAN build something sustainable.

On and on they went. Thousands of comments, most of them glowing. People tagging friends, sharing their own stories of burnout and restoration, asking about visiting hours and whether they shipped furniture.

"Look at the view count," Greg said.

Liz refreshed the page. 547,293.

"It's still going up."

They sat there, coffee cooling in their mugs, watching the numbers climb. 548,156. 549,022. Each refresh brought thousands more views.

"I don't think we understood who Jason was," Liz said finally. "How big his platform is."

"No," Greg agreed. "We definitely didn't."

Liz's phone buzzed. Then buzzed again. And again. She picked it up to find a flood of Instagram notifications. Their business account—which had maybe three hundred followers, mostly friends and locals—was suddenly exploding with new follows, comments, direct messages.

Just saw the video! Do you ship furniture?

What are your hours? Planning a trip!

That spring salad looked AMAZING. Is it still on the menu?

Do you do custom furniture restoration?

Greg's phone started buzzing too. He looked at it, then at Liz, both of them just staring at their screens for a moment.

"This is really happening," Liz said softly.

"Yeah," Greg said. "It is."

They sat there in the quiet café, phones buzzing intermittently, the morning still peaceful around them. But everything felt different now—like standing on the edge of something they couldn't quite see yet.

The video had been live for less than twenty-four hours. Whether their world was about to change, or if this was just a momentary blip of internet attention that would fade by tomorrow—they had no idea.

* * *

The fryer oil popped and hissed as Dale dropped the first batch of batter into the heat. Dale and Donna's Funnel Cakes had been open for two hours, and the Wildwood boardwalk was beginning to fill with the day's first wave of tourists. Through the open door, the smell of fried dough mixed with salt air and sunscreen.

Donna stood behind the counter, adjusting the new chalkboard for what felt like the hundredth time. She'd written "Today's Special: Nutella Dream—warm Nutella drizzle, house-made vanilla whipped cream, fresh strawberries" in careful bubble letters. She set down the chalk.

"It's perfect," Dale said from the fryers, not looking up. "Stop fussing."

"Shouldn't you be at the restaurant?" Donna asked, though she was grateful he was here.

"Eduardo has it covered. Lunch prep is done, and he can handle service." Dale glanced up with a slight smile. "I told him I needed to be here for the relaunch. This is more important right now."

The shop looked different now. Cleaner. More focused.

Gone were the cluttered promotional posters and the overwhelming menu board with thirty different topping combinations. In their place hung three simple boards: Classic Funnel Cakes, Funnel Cake Flights, and Daily Special. A small glass display case near the front window showcased the "flights"—trays with three mini funnel cakes, each topped differently.

Through the window, Donna could see families beginning their morning stroll, teenagers in swimsuits heading to the beach, couples with coffee cups walking hand-in-hand. Most walked right past their shop, eyes drawn to the flashier storefronts down the way. Her stomach tightened.

"Derek should be out there by now," she said, checking her watch.

As if on cue, Derek emerged from the back room, carrying a large tray of sample-sized funnel cake pieces, each one carefully arranged with a toothpick. He grinned at them, radiating the kind of enthusiasm only a college kid working a summer job could muster.

"Ready to make some magic happen?" he asked.

"Just remember," Dale said, finally looking up from the fryers, "you're not selling. You're sharing. Tell them what makes us different."

Derek nodded and headed out onto the boardwalk.

Annie wiped down the counter, watching through the window as Derek approached a family with small kids. "Think this is going to work?"

"It has to," Donna said quietly.

Within minutes, the first customers of the relaunch trickled in—not a flood, but a start. Through the window, Donna could see Derek working the boardwalk. Some people brushed past him without a glance, but most stopped when he offered a sample. Who could turn down free food? A middle-aged couple who'd just tried one of his samples headed straight for the shop. Donna took a breath and greeted them with a smile.

"We heard you're doing something new with local ice cream?" the woman asked, studying the menu boards.

"That's right," Donna said, feeling her confidence build. "We partnered with Boardwalk Creamery. They've been making ice cream here for twenty years—real flavors, small batches."

The man peered at the display case. "What are those? Flights?"

"Three mini funnel cakes on a tray," Dale explained, joining Donna at the counter. "You can try different flavors. We have a Classic Flight—powdered sugar, strawberry, and cinnamon sugar. Or the Premium Flight with Nutella, salted caramel, and honey butter."

"We'll try the Premium," the woman said, intrigued.

Dale prepared it with the careful attention he'd always brought to his restaurant kitchen. Three perfectly fried mini funnel cakes arranged on a tray, each topped with precision. He drizzled the warm Nutella so it pooled slightly in the ridges, added dollops of salted caramel, and finished with a pat of honey butter that began to melt on contact.

The couple took their tray to a small table by the window. Donna tried not to stare as they tried each one, but she couldn't help watching their faces. They conferred quietly between bites, and she caught fragments of their conversation.

"This is wonderful," the woman said to her husband.

Donna felt something loosen in her chest.

By mid-morning, the strategy was working. Customers who'd tried Derek's samples began trickling in. Not a flood, but steady. Real interest.

A young woman in her twenties approached the counter, slightly breathless. "Is it true you're partnering with Boardwalk Creamery? Because their brown butter pecan is literally the best ice cream I've ever had."

"It's true," Donna said. "Want to try it on a funnel cake?"

The woman ordered immediately, then pulled out her

phone to take a quick photo before digging in. Her eyes closed in appreciation.

"Oh wow," she said. "This is perfect."

By noon, they had a line. Not as long as Sugar Rush's line, but respectable. Meaningful. Dale worked the fryers while Donna and Annie handled orders, their rhythm settling into something efficient and familiar.

The Daily Special—Nutella with house-made whipped cream and fresh strawberries—was outselling their regular menu items. People kept asking what tomorrow's special would be.

Around one o'clock, during a brief lull, Donna noticed someone standing outside their window, watching. Her heart sank when she recognized him.

Frank Larson.

He stood with his arms crossed, studying the flow of customers, the display case, Derek working the boardwalk with his sample tray. His expression was unreadable, but Donna could tell he was taking it all in—counting heads, noting the interest Derek was generating.

Donna felt Dale tense beside her.

"He's noticed," Dale said quietly.

"Let him notice," Donna replied.

After another minute, Frank walked through the open doorway. He approached the counter with the easy confidence of someone who thought he owned half the boardwalk.

"Frank," Dale said evenly.

"Dale." Frank's eyes swept over the new menu boards, lingering on the Daily Special. "New setup. Doing something different, I see."

"We are," Dale said.

"Samples on the boardwalk." Frank tilted his head slightly. "Smart move. Looks like it's working."

Dale said nothing, waiting.

Frank's gaze moved to the chalkboard. "Nutella Dream.

House-made whipped cream." A slight smirk. "Sounds almost artisanal."

"It is," Donna said.

Frank looked at her, then back at Dale. "Can I try one?"

Donna and Dale exchanged glances. This felt like sizing up the competition, not a peace offering.

"Sure," Dale said finally.

Dale made the funnel cake himself, plating it with the same care he'd shown all morning. The Nutella drizzle, the whipped cream, the fresh strawberries. He handed it across the counter without a word.

Frank took the plate to a seat by the window. Donna, Dale, and Annie all pretended not to watch as he cut into the funnel cake with a fork. He took a bite, chewing slowly.

His eyes closed for just a second. Then he opened them quickly, as if catching himself. He took another bite, more deliberately this time, his jaw working as he tasted each compo-nent. Another bite. His expression softened slightly—just for a moment—before he caught himself again and his face went neutral.

When he was finished, he sat back and looked at the empty plate for a long moment. Then he stood and brought it back to the counter.

"The Nutella," Frank said, his tone carefully casual. "You warmed it?"

"Yeah," Dale said.

Frank nodded slowly. "And the cream—there's something in it. Maple?"

"Vanilla bean and maple," Dale confirmed.

Frank was quiet, seeming to debate something internally. Finally, he pulled out his wallet. "Not bad," he said, his voice deliberately offhand. "The strawberries are good. Fresh."

Dale's eyebrow raised slightly. "Thanks."

"I mean, it's still just a funnel cake," Frank added quickly, a hint of his old cockiness returning. "But..." He paused. "You know what you're doing."

Dale just nodded, accepting it without much reaction.

Donna picked up the twenty and handed it back to him. "On the house."

Frank looked at her, then at the returned bill in his hand, then pocketed it with a slight nod. "Appreciate it." He headed for the door, then paused and glanced back at Dale. "Good luck with this."

And then he was gone.

Dale stood staring at the doorway for a moment after Frank left.

"Well," Donna said quietly. "That was unexpected."

Dale nodded slowly. "Yeah. It was."

The lunch rush did hit, and it was strong. Customers who'd tried Derek's samples returned with friends. Word spread about the Boardwalk Creamery partnership. People ordered the Daily Special in droves, many asking to be put on a mailing list for future specials.

By three o'clock, they'd sold out of the Nutella special and had to improvise a new one—lemon curd with fresh blueberries and powdered sugar. It sold just as well.

When they finally closed at eight that night, Donna tallied the receipts while Dale cleaned the fryers. Annie and Derek had already gone home.

"Well?" Dale asked, wiping down the last counter.

Donna looked up from her record books, her eyes bright. "We're up forty percent from our best day last year."

Dale stopped mid-wipe. "Forty percent?"

"Forty percent," Donna confirmed. "And we have seventeen people who signed up for the Daily Special mailing list. Seventeen people who want to know what we're making tomorrow."

Dale set down his towel. "We did it."

"We did," Donna said, grabbing her keys. "I can take it from here tomorrow. You can get back to the restaurant."

Dale looked around at the shop one more time—the cleaned counters, the empty display case, the chalkboard already wiped clean for tomorrow's special. "What are you going to write up there?"

"I don't know yet," Donna said, heading for the door. "What inspires you?"

"Everything," Dale said, following her out. "Absolutely everything."

CHAPTER TEN

Sarah was zipping up her suitcase when she heard a knock on the door. Chris opened it to find Amber and Kevin standing outside.

"Breakfast at Elizabeth's?" Amber asked. "Last meal before we all head home?"

Chris looked at Sarah, who nodded.

"Sounds good," he said. "Give us five minutes?"

"Perfect! We'll wait out here."

Chris closed the door and turned to Sarah, lowering his voice. "They've really grown on us, haven't they?"

"They really have," Sarah whispered back. "I'm actually going to miss them."

Five minutes later, all four of them had checked out and left their luggage with the front desk. Coincidentally, both couples had flights in the afternoon. Amber and Kevin's was at two, Sarah and Chris's at three. Checkout was at ten, leaving them the morning to kill.

They walked together toward Elizabeth's in the Bywater, the opposite direction from the French Quarter. The morning air was already warm as they made their way through the Marigny, past colorful Creole cottages with their ornate ironwork and overgrown gardens spilling onto the sidewalks. A cat watched them from a porch swing. Someone was practicing saxophone in an upstairs apartment, the notes drifting down to the street. They crossed into the Bywater, where the houses became more eclectic with bright murals on warehouse walls, yards filled with sculptures made from scrap metal, and a corner store advertising po'boys and daiquiris. There was something bittersweet about their last morning in New Orleans.

"Last day!" Amber exclaimed, though her usual volume was dialed down a notch. She looked tired, dark circles under her eyes. "We barely slept. Things kept happening all night."

"Us too," Sarah said. "What kind of things?"

Kevin launched into a detailed account as they walked. "Doors opening and closing. Footsteps in the hallway. At one point, all our clothes fell off the hangers in the closet. Fell. As if someone had swiped them all down at once."

"We heard the trumpet again," Amber added. "Really loud this time, as if someone was playing right outside our window. But when we looked, no one was there."

"Same," Chris said. "Except in our room it was coming from inside. From the bathroom."

"The bathroom!" Amber's eyes widened. "That's where we heard it too! What if that's where he died? The jazz musician?"

They reached Elizabeth's, a colorful restaurant in the Bywater with mismatched chairs and local artwork on the walls. The host told them it would be about fifteen minutes, so they put their names in and stood near the door, swapping ghost stories while locals and tourists alike walked past with to-go cups of coffee.

"The scariest part," Kevin said, dropping his voice even though no one around them was listening, "was around one in the morning. We heard something in the common area, papers rustling. So I opened our door to look, and the guest book on the table was flipping. Pages turning on their own, fast, as if someone was rifling through it looking for something."

"No way," Chris said.

"I saw it too," Amber confirmed. "Both of us stood there watching it for about thirty seconds. Then it stopped. The book just closed itself."

Sarah felt a chill despite the warm morning. "That's legitimately terrifying."

"It was!" Amber said. "But also kind of... I don't know. Exciting? People pay good money for haunted tours in this city, and we got the real deal for free. We came to New Orleans for an experience, and we definitely got one."

"Chris, party of four!" the host called out.

They were seated in a corner table near the window, the restaurant buzzing with conversation and the smell of coffee and bacon.

"We have to get the praline bacon for the table," Amber said, not even looking at the menu. "It's required."

They ordered immediately: praline bacon to share, Sarah got the fried oyster eggs Florentine, Chris went for the Eggs Elizabeth—grilled French bread topped with ham, poached eggs, and hollandaise—Kevin ordered the cornbread waffle with duck and sweet potato hash, Amber chose the Redneck Eggs—fried green tomatoes with poached eggs and hollandaise —and she insisted they all get the Bloody Marys because "it's New Orleans, you have to."

"So what did you guys end up doing yesterday?" Amber asked once their drinks arrived.

"We just explored," Sarah said. "Walked around the Quarter, bought some souvenirs. Tried to act as if we hadn't witnessed our room being haunted."

"Same," Kevin said. "We went to that voodoo shop on Decatur Street. The woman there told us the whole French Quarter is haunted. Something about being built on old cemeteries."

"Comforting," Chris said sarcastically.

Their food arrived, and everyone focused on eating. The praline bacon was everything Sarah had heard about—thick-cut bacon coated in a caramelized pecan praline glaze, somehow both savory and sweet. Her Eggs Florentine was the New Orleans version—creamed spinach and fried oysters over potatoes, topped with poached eggs and hollandaise. Chris's Eggs Elizabeth came on thick slices of grilled French bread with ham, poached eggs, and rich hollandaise sauce. Kevin's cornbread waffle was topped with confit duck and sweet potato hash, drizzled with pepper jelly. Amber's Redneck Eggs featured crispy fried green tomatoes as the base, topped with perfectly poached eggs and hollandaise.

"This is amazing," Chris remarked, breaking into one of the poached eggs and watching the yolk run over the ham.

"Right?" Amber agreed, reaching for another piece of praline bacon. "We need to figure out how to make this at home."

"I bet we could," Kevin said. "Can't be that hard. Bacon, pecans, brown sugar?"

They ate in comfortable silence for a few minutes, savoring their food and watching the Bywater morning unfold through the window.

After finishing breakfast, the group exchanged contact information, with Amber insisting on taking one last group photo outside the restaurant.

The walk back to Maison Beaumont took them through the Bywater and into the Marigny. The morning had grown warmer, the streets busier with locals going about their day.

At the guest house, they retrieved their luggage from the front desk. Amber and Kevin's cab was already waiting at the curb.

"This was fun," Kevin said. "Safe travels, you guys."

"You too," Chris said.

They hugged goodbye—quick, friendly hugs. Then Amber

and Kevin climbed into their cab with their bags. Sarah and Chris waved as the cab pulled away.

Sarah checked her phone. "Our cab should be here in about ten minutes."

They sat on a bench in the courtyard with their luggage. In the late-morning light, it looked peaceful.

"Hard to believe we're leaving already," Sarah murmured.

"Our honeymoon went fast," Chris agreed.

They sat quietly, taking it all in one last time. The banana trees, the brick pathways, the wrought iron furniture. They listened to the sounds of the neighborhood, a saxophone from somewhere nearby, cars passing on the street, birds in the trees.

A car pulled up to the curb, and Sarah recognized it immediately.

James.

He got out, wearing the same Hawaiian shirt and the same gold chains. His grin was as wide as ever.

"The newlyweds!" he boomed. "How was the honeymoon? Did you survive the ghost?"

"Barely," Chris said, loading their bags into the trunk.

They climbed into the back seat, and James pulled away from the curb, weaving aggressively into traffic and honking at a taxi with his usual reckless confidence.

"So you heard the trumpet?" James asked, weaving through traffic.

"We heard a lot more than that," Sarah said, gripping the door handle as James took a corner fast enough to make her stomach lurch.

"Oh yeah?" He glanced at them in the rearview mirror, genuinely interested. "Tell me everything."

They did. The footsteps, the doors slamming, the lights flickering, the bathroom door swinging open and closed. The guest book pages flipping wildly in the common area at one in the morning. The clothes falling off the hangers. All of it.

James listened, nodding along, taking one hand off the

wheel to gesture enthusiastically and making Sarah's heart race every time.

"Yep, yep, that's him," James said. "That's Clarence."

"Clarence?" Chris asked.

"Clarence Oliver. That was his name. The jazz musician." James ran a red light and honked at someone who dared to honk at him first. "I told you about him, remember? Died in the thirties?"

"You said he still plays trumpet," Sarah said.

"Right, right. But I didn't tell you the whole story." James merged onto the highway, somehow accelerating and changing lanes simultaneously. "Didn't want to freak you out before you even checked in."

"What's the whole story?" Chris pressed, bracing himself against the seat as James swerved around a slow-moving sedan.

"So Clarence Oliver, he was a trumpet player. Real talented guy, played in all the clubs on Frenchmen Street back in the day. But he had a problem." James paused for dramatic effect, nearly rear-ending a pickup truck before swerving into the next lane. "He was in love with a woman who didn't love him back."

Sarah found herself leaning forward, caught up in the story despite the terror of James's driving.

"He played at her wedding," James continued. "Can you imagine? The woman he loved, marrying someone else, and he's there playing trumpet at the reception. Afterward, he went back to his room at the guest house and played his trumpet all night long. Sat there playing love songs until the sun came up."

"That's depressing," Chris said.

"It gets worse," James said cheerfully, cutting across three lanes of traffic to make their exit. "He died that night. Heart attack, right there in the room. Still holding his trumpet."

Sarah gasped softly.

"So now he's stuck there, right? Still playing his trumpet, still trying to process what happened. The locals say you can hear him every night, playing the same songs he played at her wedding. And he gets irritated when couples stay in his room because it reminds him of what he lost."

"That's why he was messing with us," Chris said.

"Exactly!" James hit the brakes hard at a red light, and Sarah flew forward, caught by her seatbelt. "He doesn't like honeymoon couples. Gets jealous. Acts out. Nothing danger-ous, mind you. He's not trying to hurt anyone. He just wants attention. Wants people to remember him."

"Well, mission accomplished," Sarah said. "We're definitely going to remember him."

"Good, good." The light turned green, and James floored it. "Most people don't believe me when I tell them the story. They think I'm just trying to spook the tourists. But you guys experienced it firsthand. You know I'm telling the truth."

They were approaching the airport now, and Sarah felt a strange mix of relief, knowing they'd survived both the haunting and James's driving, and sadness that their honey-moon was ending.

"You know what the crazy part is?" Sarah said. "I'm actu-ally glad it happened. The ghost, I mean. It made the trip... memorable."

"Memorable!" James laughed that big, booming laugh. "That's one word for it! Your friends and family are going to love this story!"

He arrived at the departures terminal, somehow finding a spot right at the curb despite the chaos of cars and buses and people with luggage. He popped the trunk and helped them unload their bags.

"Thanks for the ride," Chris said, handing him cash and what Sarah suspected was a generous tip.

"My pleasure! And hey—" James looked at both of them seriously for the first time since they'd met him. "Y'all come back to New Orleans sometime, you hear? This city's got plenty more stories for you!"

"We will," Sarah promised.

They watched him drive away, merging back into traffic with his characteristic disregard for safety, and then headed into the airport.

* * *

It had been a couple days since Bob and Judy's last trip to the lighthouse, when they'd watched those figures retrieve the metal case and bury another in a new location.

Now they sat in their living room, the evening news murmuring from the television while Judy flipped through a gardening magazine. Bob was scrolling through his phone, only half paying attention to the anchor's voice droning about traffic updates and weather forecasts.

"Coming up next," the anchor said, "authorities break up what they're calling a sophisticated smuggling operation right here in Cape May. We'll have the details after this break."

Bob's thumb stopped mid-scroll. He glanced at the TV then at Judy, who'd lowered her magazine slightly.

"Smuggling?" she said. "In Cape May?"

"That's what he said."

They sat through two minutes of commercials, including car dealerships, pharmaceutical ads, and a local real estate agent promising to sell homes fast, before the news returned. The anchor reappeared on screen, his expression serious.

"Cape May County authorities, working with the Coast Guard, have disrupted what officials are calling a well-organized smuggling ring operating along the southern shore," he said. "The operation involved the theft and transport of historical artifacts stolen from museums and private collections throughout the Mid-Atlantic."

Bob leaned forward slightly. The screen cut to footage of the beach near Cape May Point, specifically the area around Battery 223. Yellow police tape cordoned off a section of the dunes. Federal agents in windbreakers marked "HSI" and "Coast Guard" moved methodically through the sand.

"The break in the case came from an anonymous tip," the anchor continued. "Someone called the Coast Guard with specific coordinates and a detailed description of suspicious activity near the World War II bunker at Cape May Point State Park."

Judy turned to look at Bob. "Anonymous tip?"

Bob kept his eyes on the screen, but she saw the corner of his mouth twitch.

The report continued with an interview featuring a Coast Guard lieutenant commander standing on the beach, the bunker visible behind him. "The caller provided remarkably precise information," he said. "GPS coordinates, times, descriptions of individuals, even a boat registration number. That level of detail was crucial to making these arrests. This was a joint operation with Homeland Security Investigations and the FBI's Art Crime Team."

"Arrests?" Judy said. "They caught them?"

The screen showed new footage now of a small white boat with blue trim being towed by a Coast Guard vessel. Bob recognized it immediately. NJ4827ZY was visible on the hull.

"Three individuals have been taken into custody so far," the lieutenant commander said. "We believe this is part of a larger network, and we expect additional arrests in the coming weeks. We've recovered approximately two dozen artifacts that had been reported stolen over the past eighteen months. Items included Revolutionary War-era documents, Civil War memorabilia, even some Native American artifacts that had been taken from a museum in Pennsylvania."

The report cut to interior shots of what looked like a Coast Guard office, showing a table covered with plastic evidence bags, each containing documents or small objects. Bob caught a glimpse of that metal case, the hard-sided rectangular container he'd seen through his binoculars.

"The suspects were using the bunker at Cape May Point as a temporary cache," the anchor explained. "They would hide stolen items there, mark the burial locations in the dunes nearby, then coordinate retrievals with an accomplice on a boat offshore. It's believed they were transporting the artifacts up the coast for sale to private collectors."

Judy set her magazine down completely now. "Bob."

"Hmm?"

"Who called in the tip?"

Bob looked at her, his expression carefully neutral. "The report said it was anonymous."

"Bob."

He shrugged, reaching for his coffee mug on the side table. "You know, it's funny. I was looking through my phone the other day and noticed I'd called the Coast Guard. Must have been a pocket dial or something."

"A pocket dial," Judy repeated flatly. "That gave them GPS coordinates and a boat registration number."

"Weird, right?" Bob took a sip of his coffee, his eyes twinkling.

Judy stared at him for a long moment, then a slow smile spread across her face. "When did you call them?"

"Right after we got back from the lighthouse the last time we were there." Bob set his mug down. "I'd been thinking about what we saw. The coordination, the boat, that metal case. It just didn't sit right. So I looked up the Coast Guard tip line and... well, I figured it couldn't hurt to mention what we'd observed."

"You gave them everything?"

"Everything," Bob confirmed. "The boat registration I'd memorized. NJ4827ZY. The exact location where we saw them digging, about thirty yards north of the bunker. The second burial spot near those distinctive rocks, about fifty yards north. The times we'd observed activity."

On the television, the news had moved to another story, but

Judy wasn't paying attention anymore. "And you didn't tell me?"

"I wasn't sure anything would come of it," Bob said. "Didn't want to get your hopes up. For all I knew, I was calling in a geocaching club or some elaborate beach scavenger hunt."

"Some scavenger hunt," Judy said, glancing back at the TV, which was now showing footage of the arrests. "Bob, you helped bust a smuggling ring."

"We helped," Bob corrected. "You're the one who wanted to climb the lighthouse in the first place. Your idea about the stairs being good exercise."

Judy laughed. "I just wanted a workout. I didn't expect us to become amateur detectives."

"Well," Bob said, settling back into his chair with a satisfied expression, "I'd say it was the most productive exercise routine we've ever had."

They sat in comfortable silence for a moment, the evening news moving on to sports scores and weather forecasts. Bob picked up his coffee again, and Judy retrieved her magazine, but neither of them were really focused on what they were doing.

"You know," Judy said finally, "I don't know how we're going to top uncovering a smuggling operation. That's going to be a tough act to follow."

"Maybe next time we'll just enjoy the view and the exercise," Bob said. "Let the smugglers take a week off."

Judy grinned at him. "Where's the fun in that?"

Bob chuckled. They turned their attention back to the television, where the weather forecaster was predicting another beautiful day tomorrow, perfect, Bob thought, for climbing stairs and keeping an eye on the beach below.

After all, you never knew what you might see from the top of a lighthouse.

CHAPTER ELEVEN

Two days after they'd watched Jason's video, Liz stood behind the counter, a little breathless, watching the steady stream of people flow into Furnish & Feast. Cape May always had tourists, especially as the season picked up, but this was different. These people weren't just wandering in. They were arriving with phones already out, taking photos, their eyes bright with the particular excitement of people who'd come looking for something specific and found it.

"Is this the place from the video?" a woman asked, stepping up to the counter. She had her phone out, showing the YouTube thumbnail of Furnish & Feast. "The café with the furniture?"

"That's us," Liz said, trying to sound calmer than she felt.

"Oh my gosh, it's even prettier in person." The woman glanced around, taking it all in. The ribbon wall, the flickering candles, the restored furniture pieces arranged throughout the space. Then she headed toward the café to order.

Liz watched the flow of people, some browsing her furniture and décor, others making their way to the café counter for food and coffee. The two sides of the business were working in tandem, just as they'd envisioned, but at a pace neither of them had anticipated.

From across the space, she could see Greg working in the café kitchen, visible through the open area behind the marble-topped counter. He had called Charlie and Patrick in early, and all three of them were moving with the kind of focused intensity she hadn't seen since his Heirloom days.

The difference was that today, Greg was smiling.

"Two spring salads!" he called out. "Cucumber sandwiches coming up!"

The hours blurred together. Orders. Coffee. Questions about the furniture. Another wave of customers. A man paused at the refinished dresser she'd placed near the window, the one she'd finished just two days ago, the oak piece she'd stained walnut and fitted with new brass hardware.

"How much?" he asked.

She told him the price, and he didn't even hesitate. "I'll take it. Can you hold it until this afternoon? I'm staying at a B&B a few blocks away."

"Of course," she said, and placed a "SOLD" tag on top of the dresser.

At ten-thirty, the vintage armchair was gone. A young couple who'd driven down from Philadelphia specifically to visit after seeing the video bought it. An hour later, someone bought the side table she'd painted sage green, the one with the delicate turned legs that had taken her hours to sand smooth.

She glanced around her carefully curated space and felt a flutter of panic. Her furniture section was starting to look sparse. The smaller items were selling too. The vintage brass candleholders, the mercury glass vases, the throw pillows. But the actual pieces, the restored furniture that gave the space its character and substance, were disappearing faster than she could replace them.

When the lunch rush hit, she was down to two pieces, a nightstand she'd just finished staining yesterday and a wooden bench she'd been planning to reupholster but hadn't gotten to yet.

The ribbon wall had grown sparse too. Whole sections were empty, the pegs visible where spools used to hang. People were buying ribbon by the armful. "For a project," one woman explained, clutching six spools of varying patterns. "I'm wrapping gifts for a wedding, and these colors are perfect."

The place was starting to look picked over, almost empty in spots, and Liz felt the strange dual sensation of being thrilled and slightly panicked.

"Liz!" Greg called from the kitchen. "Can you run these out?"

Liz walked over to the café side where Greg had plated two sandwiches on the counter. She grabbed them. Cucumber sandwiches on his house-baked sourdough, the bread toasted golden, thin cucumber rounds layered with cream cheese and fresh dill, a sprinkle of flaky sea salt visible on top. Simple, elegant, exactly the kind of thing Greg did best.

She delivered them to a couple sitting by the window, and the woman smiled as she looked at the plate.

"This looks amazing," she said, pulling out her phone to take a photo.

Liz smiled and headed back toward the counter, but someone stopped her.

"Excuse me, do you have any more of those vintage dough bowls? The ones with the dried lavender?"

"I'm sorry, we're out of those," Liz said.

"What about the throw pillows? The blue ones?"

"Those too. But I have a few in cream if you're interested."

The woman's face fell slightly, but she nodded. "I'll take them."

The afternoon became a steady, relentless rhythm. Orders. Sales. Questions. A constant stream of transactions. Liz rang up purchases while Greg and his team worked furiously in the kitchen. The café tables were full, people waiting for seats, the low hum of conversation mixed with the clink of silverware and the hiss of the espresso machine.

Around two o'clock, Greg stepped out of the kitchen, his apron spattered, his hair damp with sweat. He crossed over to Liz's side of the shop.

"We're out of butter lettuce," he said quietly. "And radishes. And I've got maybe six portions of roasted vegetables left for the panini."

"What about the sandwiches?"

"We can do cucumber for maybe another hour. But after that..." He shook his head. "We're going to have to cut the menu down. Way down."

"How much longer can we go?"

Greg glanced back at the kitchen, did some mental calculation. "Maybe two hours at this pace. Three if it slows down."

It didn't slow down.

At three-thirty, they'd run out of focaccia. Half an hour later, the cucumber sandwiches were gone. Around four-fifteen, Greg came out of the kitchen holding a piece of paper and a roll of tape.

"We have to close early," he said. "We're completely out."

Together, they made a handwritten sign: "SOLD OUT FOR TODAY - THANK YOU! Open again tomorrow at 8 AM."

Greg taped it to the front door while Liz posted a similar message to their Instagram account. She watched the comments start rolling in almost immediately.

"Worth the wait!"

"Just finished lunch here. AMAZING."

"Driving down tomorrow. Hope you have more salads!"

The last few customers finished their meals, paid, and left, appearing satisfied and slightly dazed by the whole experience. Finally, just over an hour before their usual closing time, Liz locked the door and flipped the sign to "CLOSED."

The silence was sudden and startling.

She turned around and surveyed the space. The café tables were covered with dishes, napkins, crumpled receipts. Her side of the shop looked ransacked. Empty pegs on the ribbon wall, bare shelves where her carefully curated décor had been, two lonely furniture pieces sitting where there used to be a dozen. But despite the disorder, despite the mess, she felt a surge of pure elation.

Greg leaned against the doorframe between the café and her side of the shop. Charlie and Patrick came up behind him, both exhausted but grinning.

"Well," Greg said. "That happened."

Liz started laughing. She couldn't help it. The absurdity of it all. The line out the door, the sold-out menu, the nearly empty shelves. Greg joined her, and then Charlie and Patrick, until all four of them were standing there laughing at the whirl-wind of the day.

"Seriously," Patrick said, wiping his eyes. "That was the most orders I've ever done in a five-hour stretch."

"Thank you," Greg said, clapping Charlie on the shoulder, then Patrick. "You killed it today. Both of you."

After Charlie and Patrick left, Greg and Liz spent the next hour cleaning. They washed dishes, wiped down tables, swept the floors. Greg cleaned the kitchen while Liz straightened her remaining inventory, trying to make the sparse shelves appear intentional rather than depleted. She pulled out her phone and started making a list of what she needed to restock.

When they finally finished, they stood together in the middle of the café, surveying their work.

"We did it," Liz said softly.

"We surely did," Greg agreed.

"And we're going to be home by five-thirty," she added, glancing at the clock. "In time for dinner with the boys."

They'd talked about this so many times—how to run a business that didn't consume their lives, that left room for family dinners and weekends together. After Greg's burnout from Heirloom, after the years of sixty-hour weeks and missed moments, they'd promised themselves this would be different.

And it was. Even today, with the disorder and the line out the door and the sold-out menu, they were still closing at a reasonable hour. Still making it back for dinner with their boys.

"I need to order more ribbon," Liz said, eyeing the depleted wall. "And restock everything. And I need to find more furniture pieces to restore."

"I need to triple my vegetable order," Greg said. "And probably get more butter lettuce, more radishes. Maybe bring in extra help for the weekend."

"Can we handle this?" Liz asked, not worried exactly, just... wondering.

Greg surveyed the space—the café, the furniture shop, the dream they'd created together. "I think we can. It's not like Heirloom. We're not trying to be a destination fine dining restaurant. We're just... this. A café and a furniture shop. Simple."

"It didn't feel simple today."

"No," he admitted. "But we had boundaries. We're closing at a reasonable hour. We'll be home in time for family dinner. We're not sacrificing everything for this."

Liz leaned into him, feeling the truth of it. The exhaustion was different this time: satisfying rather than depleting. The success felt manageable rather than overwhelming.

"I think we can do this," she said. "Really do this."

"Yeah," Greg said. "I think so too."

They locked up and walked to the car, the evening air warm and pleasant, Cape May starting to settle into its evening rhythm. On the drive home, Liz pulled out her phone and saw an email notification from Jason Potter.

She opened it.

Hey Liz and Greg!

Just wanted to check in and see how things are going post-video. I've been watching the engagement numbers and they're still climbing. People are really responding to your story.

Hope the video is bringing you some good business. Let me know how it goes!

Best, Jason

Liz read it aloud to Greg, then started typing a response.

Jason,

Good business is an understatement. We had a line out the door from the moment we opened. Sold out of almost all our food by 4:15 PM. Liz's furniture pieces are flying off the shelves—she's down to two pieces from a dozen. We had to close early because we literally ran out of everything.

It's incredible. And a little overwhelming. But we're figuring it out.

Thank you. Truly. This video changed everything for us. We're so grateful.

Liz and Greg

She hit send and watched Greg navigate the familiar streets toward home. Through the car window, she could see other families—people finishing their workdays, kids playing in yards, someone watering their garden. Normal life. The life they got to have now, too.

Her phone buzzed with Jason's response almost immediately.

That's amazing. Seriously, I'm thrilled for you both. And you should know—this video is my highest-viewed one yet. 750K views and climbing. I think it resonated because your story is real. It's about people creating something sustainable and meaningful, not just chasing growth for growth's sake.

You've inspired me, actually. I want to do more videos like this—featuring businesses that are doing it right, whether they're new like yours, or old establishments that need a boost, or people starting over after a setback. There's something powerful about showing people what's possible when you combine craft and authenticity.

Thanks for letting me tell your story. Keep me posted on how things go. And don't let the success change what makes Furnish & Feast special.

—Jason

Liz read it aloud, then glanced over at Greg. He was smiling, one hand on the wheel, the other reaching over to squeeze hers.

They pulled into their driveway, and Liz could see lights on in the house, the TV flickering in the living room window. One of their boys walked past, probably heading to the kitchen. Normal. Beautiful. Theirs.

They got out of the car and walked toward the front door together, both of them tired and happy and ready for dinner with their family. The business was booming. The video was a massive success. And they were home by five-thirty, just like they'd planned.

It wasn't just that Furnish & Feast was working.

It was that their life was working too.

* * *

Lisa arrived at Delaney's Irish Pub & Grill just after six, having walked down Washington Street Mall from where she'd parked near Ocean Street. She'd been back from San Diego for less than eight hours, her mind still processing everything that had happened in California. The flight had landed at Philadelphia International around noon, and she'd driven straight back to Cape May, her car practically steering itself while her thoughts remained three thousand miles away.

The pedestrian mall had been busy with early-evening shoppers, couples peering into storefront windows, families with soft serve cones from Kohr Brothers, a few tourists browsing the racks of Cape May sweatshirts outside Great White Shark. She'd passed Bath Time with its window display of handmade soaps and exotic lotions, the scents of lavender and sea salt drifting out whenever someone opened the door. The smell of fresh waffle cones mingled with the briny ocean air that always managed to reach even here, three blocks from the beach. String lights were just beginning to twinkle in the trees that lined the mall, and the May evening felt soft and golden, the kind of light that made everything look like a postcard.

Inside Delaney's, the warm glow of pendant lights illuminated dark wood paneling and brass fixtures. The dinner crowd was just starting to filter in. Couples at tables near the windows, a few regulars at the bar watching a Phillies game on the television above the taps. Lisa spotted Nick in a booth near the bar, and her chest tightened. He was staring down at his phone, his jaw tight with concentration, the light catching the angles of his face.

"Hey," she said, sliding into the booth across from him.

He looked up, and his face transformed—worry lines smoothing as he broke into a genuine smile. "Hey." He leaned forward across the table to kiss her quickly before settling back.

"So?" He searched her face. "How did it go?"

"It was good. Better than I expected, actually." Lisa set her phone on the table. "It all happened so fast last night. I didn't get a chance to call. But tell me what's going on with you first. You sounded stressed when you texted."

A waitress appeared before Nick could answer. "What can I get you folks?"

"Guinness," Nick said.

"Same," Lisa said. "And the fish and chips for me."

"I'll have that too," Nick said.

"You got it." The waitress disappeared toward the bar.

Nick rubbed his face with both hands. "So, I got the results from the marine biologist this afternoon."

Lisa leaned forward. "And?"

"It's something called SUMS. Sudden Unusual Mortality Syndrome." He let out a long breath. "It's real, it's documented, but it's not well understood. The biologist said it's basically a perfect storm of stress factors, the cold snap we had three weeks ago that I didn't think was that big of a deal, some bacterial issues in the water, low oxygen levels. All of it combined just... overwhelmed the oysters' immune systems."

"But you can treat it, right?" Lisa asked.

Nick shook his head. "There's no treatment. It just has to run its course. The good news is that it won't spread to new beds. It's not contagious. But the beds that are affected?" He paused. "I'm going to lose about forty percent of this season's crop. Maybe more."

"Nick, I'm so sorry."

"Yeah. But I've been thinking about it. I can apply for state disaster relief. There are programs for aquaculture farmers who experience losses from natural events. And I've been wanting to expand anyway. I talked to the marine resources office today, and there's adjacent lease area available. If I can increase my acreage by twenty-five or thirty percent, I can make up for some of the loss next season."

Lisa felt relief wash over her. "So you have a plan."

"I have a plan," Nick confirmed. "It's going to be tight this year, but I'll survive it. And honestly? Maybe it's the push I needed to scale up. I've been playing it safe, staying small. This is forcing me to think bigger."

Their beers arrived, two dark pints with perfect foam heads. Nick picked his up and took a long drink.

"The marine police called too," he continued. "They tracked down the guy who placed the crab traps. Turns out he's just some recreational crabber from Wildwood who comes down here on weekends. He had no idea he was on my lease area. He apologized, said he'd never do it again."

Lisa watched his face. "What about the cut buoy lines?"

"Storm damage." Nick shrugged. "Remember that bad storm two weeks ago? That's what did it. The lines didn't get cut. They got torn up by debris in the water. And the moved markers? The conservation officer said there've been reports of recreational boaters running through this area, not realizing they're supposed to stay in the channel. They probably knocked them around without even noticing."

"So it wasn't sabotage," Lisa said quietly.

"Nope." Nick set his glass down. "Just bad luck and nature. I saw malice where there was just... chaos. Random chance. A cold snap, some bacteria, low oxygen, careless boaters, and a guy who likes to catch crabs on weekends." He met her eyes. "I convinced myself someone was out to get me. That there was some conspiracy. But it was just a bunch of unrelated things happening at once."

Their fish and chips arrived. Golden battered cod, thick-cut fries, little containers of tartar sauce and malt vinegar. Nick picked up a fry but didn't eat it, just turned it over in his fingers.

"The biologist was actually really kind about it. She said she sees it all the time. Farmers looking for patterns, trying to find someone to blame. It's human nature. We want problems to have clear villains and clear solutions." He shook his head. "But sometimes the villain is just... water temperature and bad timing."

Nick leaned back against the booth. "OK, enough about my oysters. Tell me about San Diego. How did it go?"

Lisa took a breath. This was the moment. "It went really well. Better than I expected, actually."

"Yeah?"

"They offered me $2.3 million for Current Culture. Plus a three-year contract as creative director with a $150,000 annual salary." The numbers still felt unreal coming out of her mouth.

Nick's eyes widened. "Wow, Lisa."

"I know."

"That's... that's incredible. Did you..." He paused, watching her closely. "What did you tell them?"

"I said yes."

Nick's face broke into a huge smile, and he reached across the table for a high five. "Lisa, that's amazing!"

She met his hand with a satisfying smack. "The paperwork takes about six weeks. But they want me to start by mid-July."

"So you're moving to California?" Nick asked.

"Actually, no." Lisa couldn't help but smile. "That was one of my non-negotiables. I negotiated into my contract that I can work from here, from New Jersey. I only have to go out to San Diego once a month for meetings and product development sessions."

Nick's expression shifted from concern to relief. "Really?"

"Really. They want me at headquarters for the creative director role, working directly with their product development team, overseeing the expansion of the eco-friendly line. But I told them I do my best work here, and that if they wanted me, they had to let me stay." She was talking faster now, the words tumbling out. "I negotiated hard on the environmental standards too. They agreed to let me maintain full control over materials and suppliers for the Current Culture products. And they're creating a new position on their board—Director of Sustainability—and they want me to fill it after my three-year contract is up."

"That's huge," Nick said. "So you're staying in Cape May?"

"Yeah. And actually, I'm thinking of buying a place here. Now that I have the financial stability, I can finally stop renting month-to-month."

Nick looked at her, a small smile playing at his lips. "Why would you buy? I've got that whole bay house. Maybe... we could move in together?"

Lisa's smile widened. "You've been thinking about this?"

"For a while now, actually. Just been looking for the right time to bring it up." He grinned. "Figured this was as good a time as any."

"We should talk about that," Lisa said, her smile genuine. "But yeah... I'd really love that."

They sat like that for a moment, both smiling, the noise of the pub swirling around them. The Phillies game on TV, conversations from nearby tables, the clink of glasses at the bar. Lisa thought about the life taking shape in front of her: a national brand, financial security, a home with Nick in Cape May. Nick thought about the expansion ahead. The new lease area, the disaster relief application, the woman across from him. And how sometimes the best things happened when you stopped worrying about control and just let life unfold. Neither of them said anything, but they didn't need to. Everything they needed to say was already understood.

CHAPTER TWELVE

The farmhouse looked picture-perfect on Saturday afternoon. Margaret had arranged fresh peonies throughout the house, while Dave had mowed and set up the farm table on the back patio beneath the pergola. The May gardens were in full glory —lettuce and peas in the vegetable beds, young tomato plants staked and promising, squash vines just beginning to spread, pepper plants still small but healthy. Roses climbed the arbor, coral and pink blooms heavy on their stems, and irises bordered the stone pathways.

The farm stand near the driveway held their first harvest—radishes, mixed lettuce, fresh herbs, and sugar snap peas. Margaret had hung a sign reading "Fresh From Our Garden."

"They're here," Harper called from the front window.

Margaret smoothed her dress and headed outside with Dave. Mary and Rob's car pulled into the long gravel driveway first, followed by Billy and Delores, then Gloria and Grant with their teenagers. Valerie and Artie brought up the rear, their car packed with what looked like enough wine for a small army.

"Wow," Mary breathed as she stepped out of the car, taking in the sprawling property. "This is gorgeous."

"It's like a different world from the beach house," Valerie

said, turning in a slow circle to take it all in. The farmhouse stood tall and proud with its wraparound porch inviting and welcoming.

"Welcome to our home," Dave said, genuine pride in his voice. "We're so glad you could come."

Billy whistled low, looking around at the gardens, the barn in the distance. "This is some operation you've got here."

Dave led them on a walking tour, starting with the vegetable gardens. He explained their rotation system, showed them the asparagus beds and berry bushes. The group wandered the paths, admiring the organization and abundance.

"This is incredible," Artie said. "How do you keep up with all this?"

"We love it," Dave answered simply. "This is what we've always wanted."

They moved to the flower gardens, where the peonies stole the show. Delores gasped at the massive blooms.

"I've never seen peonies this size," she said. "What's your secret?"

"Patience and bone meal." Margaret laughed. "And these plants were here when we bought the place. They're probably thirty years old."

Gloria's teenagers had wandered toward the barn with Harper and Abby. The adults followed, and Dave opened the wide doors to reveal old beams overhead, riding equipment neatly organized, and the faint smell of hay and leather.

Grant looked around. "Do you have horses?"

"Not yet," Dave said. "But someday."

From the barn, they walked to the tree farm. The evergreens stood in neat rows at various stages of growth. Dave explained how they'd just taken over the operation—they'd keep the Christmas tree areas managed and ready for customers, while letting the other areas remain forested for nature and wildlife.

"That's brilliant," Rob said. "The location is perfect."

They strolled the tree rows, discussing varieties and growth rates. The May breeze carried the scent of new growth and freshly turned earth.

"This is so peaceful," Valerie said quietly. "I can see why you love it here."

Dave smiled, and Margaret noticed the particular contentment that settled over him here. This was his element—the land, the growing things, the quiet satisfaction of building something that would last.

By the time they returned to the house, the sun was still high in the sky, casting warm afternoon light across the property. Dave fired up the grill while Margaret brought out platters of marinated chicken and vegetables from their garden. They ate around the long farm table, passing dishes family-style, the conversation flowing easily.

"So the lock is working well?" Billy asked.

"Really well," Dave said. "We installed it this past week. It's nice to finally have that boundary in place."

"Best decision we made," Margaret added. "And we're finding a better rhythm between both places too. We realized we don't have to be at the beach every single weekend. This is home too."

"That's smart," Mary said. "You'll burn out otherwise."

As the afternoon stretched into evening, they moved to the patio furniture arranged around the fire pit. Dave built a fire while the kids explored the gardens in the golden light. The adults settled into comfortable conversation, wine glasses in hand, the firelight flickering between them.

Margaret looked around at their guests—these new friends who'd welcomed them so warmly into the beach community—now here at the farmhouse, admiring what she and Dave had built. She caught Dave's eye across the fire, and he smiled at her, that genuine smile she'd fallen in love with all those years ago. This was what they'd been searching for—all of it. The farmhouse and the beach house, the old friends and the new, the careful balance between the life they'd built and the life they were creating. They'd figured it out, finally. Two homes, one life, and enough space for it all.

* * *

It was early evening when Sarah and Chris turned onto Sunset Beach Road. They were back from New Orleans now, settling into their routines, but this was their first time returning to Sunset Beach since the wedding. Sarah rolled down her window, letting in the salt air, so different from the humid thickness of New Orleans. Crisp. Familiar. Home.

Chris pulled into the parking lot. The lot was busy, filling up with the dinner crowd and people arriving early for the sunset.

Sarah climbed out, stretching her legs. She was ready to be here, on this beach, in this place that had witnessed the beginning of everything.

They kicked off their shoes near the parking lot and walked barefoot across the sand. It was warm and pleasant, the heat of the day already starting to fade. The bay opened up before them, vast and peaceful, its surface catching the golden light of early evening.

"God, I missed this," Sarah said, breathing in deeply.

Chris took her hand. "Me too. Don't get me wrong—New Orleans was incredible. But there's something about this place."

They walked in silence for a bit, their feet making soft impressions in the sand. The beach was quieter than usual—an older couple walking hand in hand near the water's edge, a woman with a sketch pad, sitting cross-legged in the sand, someone flying a colorful kite that danced against the dimming sky. The concrete ship was visible down the beach, a familiar landmark that Sarah realized she'd stopped really seeing years ago, the way you stop noticing things that are always there.

Sarah bent down, catching the glint of something in the sand. A Cape May diamond. She picked it up, rubbing her thumb across its surface. The small quartz stone felt like sea glass in her hand, worn by endless tides.

"Found one already," she said, holding it up for Chris to see.

"Of course you did." He crouched beside her, scanning the sand. "You've always had an eye for these things."

They started walking again, both of them watching the sand now, occasionally bending to pick up stones. It was meditative, this searching. No pressure, no goal other than the simple act of looking. Sarah found three more in quick succession, holding them loosely in her cupped hand. Chris found one that was almost perfectly round, which he declared was good luck.

"Remember when we got married here?" Sarah said with a smile. "I know, I know—it wasn't that long ago."

"Feels like ancient history though," Chris said. "In a good way. Like we've already lived a whole lifetime since then."

Sarah thought about the rain-soaked ceremony, about standing here in this exact spot while the sky opened up and everyone ran for cover. About choosing to keep going anyway, to finish what they'd started despite the chaos. It seemed fitting, somehow, that their first trip back here as a married couple would be in much better weather.

"We should have brought Amber and Kevin," she said.

Chris laughed. "Can you imagine? Amber would be telling everyone on the beach about every diamond she found. Kevin would probably have a spreadsheet ranking them by size and clarity."

"With color-coded categories for different quality levels."

"And they'd be yelling across the beach every time they found one."

Sarah found herself laughing harder than the joke warranted, but it felt good. Everything felt good right now. The sand between her toes, the weight of her rings on her finger—she'd been checking obsessively since the incident in New Orleans—the easy way Chris's hand fit in hers.

Their honeymoon had been unforgettable. More than that—it had been extraordinary. The ghost stories they could now tell at dinner parties. The amazing food. The music. The dancing. The sheer chaos of Amber and Kevin and Captain Gus and James's driving. All of it felt like something they'd earned together.

"I'm hungry," Chris said. "Fish House?"

Sarah looked up at the restaurant perched at the edge of the beach, its deck extending out over the sand. "Read my mind."

They made their way back to where they'd left their shoes, brushed the sand off their feet, and headed up to the restaurant. The hostess seated them at a table on the deck with a perfect view of the bay. The sun was lower now, painting everything in shades of gold and pink.

They picked up their menus, scanning the familiar options. The waitress came by, and they ordered without hesitation. Lobster roll for Chris, salmon salad for Sarah, a bottle of white wine to share.

They sat in comfortable silence, watching the bay. The water was calm, reflecting the deepening colors of the sky. A few gulls wheeled overhead, their calls carrying on the breeze. In the distance, Sarah could see a line of pelicans flying low over the water in perfect formation.

The waitress returned with their wine, pouring two glasses. Sarah took a sip, savoring the crisp, cool taste.

"This is nice," Sarah said. "Just... this."

"This is perfect," Chris agreed.

Their food arrived, and Sarah took her first bite of salmon, perfectly grilled and sitting on a bed of fresh greens. Chris took a bite of his lobster roll and nodded approvingly. For a few minutes, they just ate, occasionally sharing bites, watching the sun sink lower.

"You know what's weird?" Sarah said, spearing a piece of salmon with her fork. "I loved New Orleans. I really did. But I think I love being home more."

Chris nodded. "I was thinking the same thing on the drive back. It's good to have adventures, but it's better to have a place you want to come back to."

"Very philosophical, Chris."

They lingered over their meal, in no rush to leave. The sun was getting close to the horizon now, and Sarah could see more people starting to arrive on the beach, claiming spots to watch the sunset. It was one of the things Cape May was known for —the sunsets over the Delaware Bay were spectacular, and people came from all over to witness them.

"Should we get dessert?" Chris asked as their waitress cleared their plates.

"We should definitely get dessert," Sarah said. "When in Rome. Or, you know, when at the beach where you got married."

They ordered the homemade ice cream to share and fresh coffee. The ice cream arrived quickly, served in a bowl they could split, and they took turns with their spoons.

"This is almost as good as those beignets," Sarah said.

"Almost," Chris agreed. "But nothing's as good as beignets covered in approximately seven pounds of powdered sugar."

The sun touched the horizon, and Sarah watched as the sky began its transformation. First gold, then orange, then streaks of pink and purple bleeding across the clouds. The water reflected it all back, creating a mirror image that made it impossible to tell where the bay ended and the sky began.

"I'll never get tired of this view," Sarah said softly.

"Me neither."

They sat together, Chris's hand finding Sarah's, their

wedding bands catching the last glint of sunlight as the sun disappeared below the horizon, leaving the sky painted in deepening shades of purple and blue. Down on the beach, Cape May diamonds caught the fading light, scattered across the sand like tiny pieces of captured sunset, small treasures waiting to be found.

Margaret spotted Mary first, walking toward them on the sidewalk with a canvas tote bag slung over her shoulder. It was a warm afternoon, and Margaret and Dave had convinced Harper and Abby to join them for a walk down Jackson Street before dinner. The girls were a few steps ahead, both on their phones, occasionally looking up to comment on a house or point something out to each other.

"Mary!" Margaret called out, waving.

Mary looked up and smiled, changing course to meet them on the corner. Harper and Abby had drifted over to look at a vintage car parked in someone's driveway.

"Margaret, Dave. Beautiful evening for a walk."

"It really is," Margaret agreed. "Perfect spring weather. What about you?"

"Just coming back from the library board meeting," Mary said. "Which, speaking of, have you two noticed all the activity around town lately? The trucks, the people measuring things, all the equipment being moved around?"

Margaret and Dave exchanged a glance. They had noticed. Hard not to, really. For the past week, there had been an unusual amount of activity around Cape May. Trucks with out-of-state plates, crews with clipboards surveying various locations, equipment being unloaded near Washington Street Mall.

"We thought maybe it was some kind of construction project," Dave said. "New utility work or something?"

Mary shook her head, her eyes bright with excitement. "Much better than that. I finally figured it out today. There was a formal announcement this morning—apparently it's been in the works for months, but they kept it quiet until everything was confirmed." She paused for dramatic effect. "Cape May is hosting a major traveling art festival. Starts in two weeks."

"An art festival?" Margaret said.

"Not just any art festival," Mary continued, clearly pleased to be the one sharing the news. "It's called Luminous. It's one of those massive outdoor installations that takes over an entire location. You know, like the light shows at Longwood Gardens or Grounds for Sculpture, but this one travels. It's only in each city for two weeks before moving on."

"I've heard of those," Dave said. "They're supposed to be incredible."

"This one is," Mary said. "I looked it up as soon as I heard. There's going to be art installations all over town. They'll be on the beach, in gardens, on street corners, in front of historic buildings. Some of it is traditional sculpture, but the big draw is the light installation. They've brought in this famous artist from Germany who does these massive light displays. Apparently his work has been featured all over Europe."

Margaret tried to picture it. Cape May, already beautiful with its Victorian architecture and beaches, transformed into an outdoor art gallery. "That sounds amazing. Why Cape May?"

"Tourism board pitched it, I think," Mary said. "They wanted to do something different, attract a new crowd. And apparently the festival organizers loved the idea of setting up in a historic beach town. They've been scouting locations for months." She shifted her tote bag to her other shoulder. "The announcement said there will be live music, food vendors, the whole thing. Some of the artists will be here in person for talks and demonstrations. It's supposed to be one of the biggest cultural events we've had in years."

"Two weeks," Dave said thoughtfully. "That's going to bring in a lot of people."

"Exactly what the town is hoping for," Mary said. "Summer is already busy, but this should draw a different crowd—art lovers, culture enthusiasts. Though I imagine some of the locals will have mixed feelings about even more crowds."

"Have they said which locations they're using?" Margaret asked.

"Some of them," Mary said. "The beach, obviously. Congress Hall is hosting something in their courtyard. There's going to be a major installation near the lighthouse. And they're still finalizing agreements with private property owners who want to participate. I imagine they'll be looking for prominent locations in historic neighborhoods. Houses with good curb appeal."

Margaret tried to picture the town transformed by art and light.

"That sounds incredible," Dave said.

"I thought so too," Mary agreed. She checked her watch. "I should get going. Rob's expecting me home for dinner, but I wanted to mention it since I figured you two would be interested."

"Thanks for filling us in," Margaret said.

Mary gave a little wave and continued down the sidewalk toward her house.

Margaret watched her go then glanced at Dave. He caught her look and smiled.

"Interesting summer ahead," he said.

Margaret nodded, already imagining the possibilities.

$$* \quad * \quad *$$

Pick up book 19 in the Cape May Series, **Cape May Beach Bums,** to follow Margaret, Liz, Dave, and the rest of the bunch.

Start book 1 in my new Ocean City series, **A Summer in Ocean City.**

Coming soon! A **Sea Isle City** series.

ABOUT THE AUTHOR

Claudia Vance is a writer of Women's Fiction and Clean Romance. She writes feel good reads that take you to places you'd like visit with characters you'd want to get to know.

She lives with her boyfriend and 2 cats in a charming small town in New Jersey, not too far from the beautiful beach town of Cape May. She worked on television shows and film sets for many years. She's an avid gardener and nature lover.